John Goldie

The Poor and Their Happiness

missions & mission philanthropy

John Goldie

The Poor and Their Happiness
missions & mission philanthropy

ISBN/EAN: 9783337406660

Printed in Europe, USA, Canada, Australia, Japan

Cover: Foto ©Andreas Hilbeck / pixelio.de

More available books at **www.hansebooks.com**

THE POOR AND THEIR HAPPINESS

The Poor and Their Happiness

MISSIONS

&

MISSION PHILANTHROPY

BY

JOHN GOLDIE

London

MACMILLAN AND CO.

AND NEW YORK

1895

CONTENTS

THE POOR AND THEIR HAPPINESS

CHAPTER I

Introductory : dealing with the inability of religion or sentiment to affect the Poor—Comparison of Missions and the Salvation Army—Natural law.

THESE pages are written throughout on the bases of Natural Law. For the amelioration, or improvement, in the condition of the Poor, we can no longer put any faith in those virtues that have been so long looked upon as the proper regenerators of mankind —Religion, Morality, Education. Nor can we include in our philanthropy, what have been considered the leaven and essence of philanthropy—Ideality, Sentiment, Imagination, or what goes to form our higher conceptions of life.

The Poor, though well acquainted with all these things, do not find them in any way useful to them in the battle of life, and as they must themselves be the principal agents in their redemption, their sympathy and co-operation must first be obtained before we can hope for success in our philanthropical efforts. Such co-operation can only be gained when the Poor have perfectly satisfied themselves of the advantages to them personally of the plan to be adopted ; and in their judgment of any scheme there are three

B

important points to be considered, viz. : How much
better will it be when adopted, over the present
condition of things? How much trouble will it take to
adopt it? and, To what extent will it disturb, or work in,
with our present habits? Which, strange to say, are
the very questions the most cultivated classes put
before themselves, when asked to modify, or adopt,
some new form of life. It is Natural law.

The Poor put no reliance upon the religious or
intellectual side of human nature as instruments to
contend with misfortune. The philanthropists believe
that they do not know what they are rejecting. It has
been the constant wail of the philanthropists that if
only the Poor would hearken to religion, or cultivate
their minds, so as to know the Divine power of the one,
or the strengthening, elevating influence of the other,
they would seek no other guides to their happiness.
Unfortunately for this view of the case, among the
Poor are a class, the most hopeless because the most
perfectly helpless of all the different varieties of poverty
that come to the gutter, who have exactly the
experience the philanthropist has longed for. These
are the droppings, the sediment from the higher classes.
All of them have had the usual religious training from
their childhood up; all have had what is called a
liberal and intellectual education. Some have come
from the manse itself; many of them can add letters
after their names. In these the Poor have an object
lesson. The forces that they have been told so persistently had power to raise them from their lowly state,
had not the power to arrest the descent of these hapless
brethren, not even at the first sign of motion, when the
strength of a child's hand should have been sufficient.
But do these educated unfortunates rely upon their religion or intellectuality to help them to contend with their
distress? No. They get rid of them, so far as they can,

and become as the people with whom their lot is cast. They find situations requiring education are filled by a class more poorly paid than the day labourer, and yet who have to wear respectable clothes, clean linen, and polished boots. It were infinitely better to wear fustian, and live as you chose on four shillings a day, than be a clerk on twenty shillings a week! They find that it was not the religion itself that they loved, as they thought it was, but the ostentation of it, and here no person cares whether they go to church or not. They have not the clothes—why should they bother? And that is an end of it.

The question may be asked, Why those things to which the better classes attach so much importance, as to make them the guiding principles of their lives, and a never ending source of enjoyment, cannot be made of the same service to the Poor? There are many we know, who never looked at the question in such a light, believing always that there can be no difference. It is therefore best at this early stage we should put our readers in possession of our experience.

Religion and mental cultivation do not take root in the social scale so low as the stratum of the Poor. There is a law in Nature of "equivalents" which we have touched upon in another chapter (Chap. III) by which we all expect a distinctly profitable return for our actions; and it is not until we rise in the social scale to that class to whom religion and cultivation are profitable do we find them cultivated. And as we have stated, where they are found below that class they are allowed to stagnate as useless weapons. These virtues did not originate among the Poor, and flow upward; they came from the leisured classes, and in their spreading downwards, they come to barren and sterile soil, where they do not grow naturally. Neither do they grow equally, religion descending further than intellectuality, because of its persistent propagation, and the many temptations held out to make it profitable.

It cannot be denied that the outward show of religion is profitable, otherwise we would not have so many impostors and hypocrites. But it is hardly conceivable how deeply the element of profit is interwoven with it, even to those who believe themselves sincere and single-minded. We will take the case of a gentleman earnestly and conscientiously imbued with religious feeling. That Religion should be absolutely and wholly its own reward to him, he takes no part in any religious service, public or private. He never speaks about it, or permits himself to be drawn into argument upon the subject. As far as he is concerned he will do no action that would infer to his fellow men that he is religious, so that they will not base their opinion of him from his religion. We know such a person. He has told us that after all, his religion is not allowed to be to him its own reward. His actings with all with whom he comes in contact are so just and upright, his promises so scrupulously fulfilled, and his whole bearing showing so much more consideration for others rather than himself, that instead of passing for a non-religious person, he has the reputation of being the most religious person in his neighbourhood. We asked him what profit he derives from this reputation ? He said it would be hard to tell in words : a hundred little kindly services every day; his slightest wish is scrupulously regarded ; he is made the arbiter of almost every quarrel and dispute, and his influence always goes for peace. Numerous responsibilities are thrust upon him unsolicited, from the people's confidence in his rectitude. In fact, he said, half-seriously, half-playfully, if he wished he might entrust his happiness to these willing neighbours, and not be in any way disappointed.

When secret religion—or that which is as near secret as well can be—is so openly rewarded, made so personally advantageous, what must the usual public exhibition of it be, as it is at present? To the great bulk of this Protestant country it is only the public acts that are worth observing; and why? Because it is only through our public worship that our social and commercial reputation can be fostered. So little do we believe a man would take the trouble of private religion, that when we hear of such a case, we are sceptical, and suspect him of some ulterior design. Now in descending through the classes, religion stops where its ostentation ceases to be socially profitable. Strange to say, that class is the most religious of all the classes as regards regularity of public attendance. Thus the most careful in religious observation lies next to a class almost wholly indifferent to it. The reason is simple—to the one it is the principal mark of class distinction; to the other it is not.

The class we refer to—the lowest of the religious classes—is the small shop-keeper, the better paid workman (the foreman and draughtsman), and the clerk. All these people come in contact with the better classes—their master and his customers, on whom their success in life depends; and the easiest acquired reputation for respectability is by religious observance. The small shop-keeper has not the capital to do an independent trade with the public like the larger ones; he has to depend upon his reputation with the few who deal with him. The clerk is continually in his master's presence, and must have a character; and the foremen and skilled workmen are being continually consulted, and must have a reputation that can bear inspection. But the common workman only comes in contact with the foreman, to whom he owes nothing but his work, and towards whom he holds a pretty independent manner. He gets neither overtime nor larger wages for being religious, and therefore he does not take the trouble.

Having been among, and having studied the ways of, the workman all our lives, we have seen this natural evolution, not once, but twenty times :—A wild and harum-scarum workman—all the best men are generally wild, because they know they always get a preference, and are never long without employment—this workman, boastful of his independence, caring as he says for neither man nor devil, leads a very irregular life. By and bye, he is suddenly made under-foreman. This produces a slight change in him, while he is protesting there is no change. But if he does not want to return to the ranks, he has to be more regular ; he has always to be in a position that he can be called up for consultation. He becomes more serious, and he has no time for larks at night. In a short time he is made a full-fledged foreman. With his increased wage he can afford to live in a better class of house. His wife chooses a house in the centre of the class to which she now aspires, and this class are a church-going people. If she wants to make acquaintances for herself and daughters, as she does, she must go to church (never a disagreeable thing to women) ; but he must also, and there you are ! Without a missionary, without an item of religious awakening, without having to open a Bible, a man becomes a Christian because it is the social habit of the class he has just joined.

The intellectual stratum is not so low as the religious one. It lacks the element of profit from public exhibition. To find it we have to rise to that class where it is a necessity. A virtue that is not publicly profitable is only cultivated as a necessity. This may seem very hard upon the virtuous, who have always very superior reasons for their actions. But virtue requires cultivation, long and weary hours of study in the early stages without any recompense of pleasure, and Nature objects to the expenditure of labour for a deferred pleasure, if a present one of equal value can be obtained. The thousands who arrange at some part of their lives to take up for the winter a special study, some going in for art, some for music, some for languages, others again going to have a serious course of mathematics, chemistry, microscopy, and who throw the whole thing up after two or three lessons, are examples of this rule. The pleasure proposed to be derived from the final acquisition of their subject becomes less and less as the hours of study are increased, until it cannot compete with some trifling pleasure of the hour. We must look for cultivation then, either in the classes who born and brought up in it in youth remain in its environment, or to those who have the time for it and to whom it is a necessity.

In the upward progression of the social scale, no fact is more notorious than that the hours of labour shorten and their reward or remuneration increases. Put in another way, the hours of leisure steadily increase, and in proper proportion the means wherewith to enjoy them, as we rise in the social scale. This is as it should be, because it is our leisure that is the most important part of our lives, and also the most expensive. Among the ordinary business classes this rule holds good. There are two notable exceptions. There are some businesses that have long hours, and yet are very profitable. The people engaged in these trades have short leisures, and plenty of money to spend them with. Because of this circumstance these people are called "common," "vulgar," and "degraded," and they certainly are illiterate. Why? Because with their money they can purchase the pleasures of a higher class than their own, while they have neither the manners nor the breeding of that class ; they therefore make an unfavourable contrast when they come in juxtaposition with its members. They are common, because the superiority of the class above them is seldom shown to them

with either the good taste or good sense that should
belong to such a class, and they are driven, when thus
insulted and angered, to assert their position on a purely
money basis. Their shortness of time and length of
purse turn them to games of chance and excitement—
gambling, betting, racing, dog-, cock-, or man-fighting.
Anything that will crush the most excitement into the
shortest time, regardless of cost. They are illiterate
because every person would rather purchase their
pleasure than make it. Mental cultivation is a home-
made means to pleasure, and consumes much time in
the making of it. They have not the time to make it,
and they have the means of purchasing other forms.

On the other hand there is a class whose fortune, or
misfortune, it is to be the very opposite of the foregoing
one. They have short hours, but they have not the
means of enjoying their long leisure in the common and
traditional manner. How then can they kill that time
between labour and sleep, so deadly to the pockets of
all of us? By study—the cheapest and best amusement
in the world. The young men of all the professions, of
the civil service, of the banks, insurance companies,
and such like ; young men who receive a small salary
rising by infinitesimal degrees through a long period
of years ; some receiving no salary, some paying a
premium for the honour of being there ;—without
private means—and few of them have any—how could
these young men put in an existence, if it were not for
books, for literature, for art, all of which can be had
for next to nothing ? Do not imagine it is an innate
love of learning that bothers these young men, it is only
a want of cash. Give the most enthusiastic among them
a hundred or two a year more of salary, and in twelve
months see how he has been prosecuting his studies.
The theatre, the music-hall and the supper-room will
have received the most of that year's income.

A clergyman had two sons, and they were brought
up as lads with a similarity of tastes in all things, as if
they had been twins.   One was placed in a bank where
he had not much to do, and almost nothing to get at
the end of the month as the reward of his exertions.
But he got home very regularly about five o'clock in
the evening.   He had to find something to do between
five and eleven, without almost a stiver to do it on.   But
there was his father's library ; there were all the young
men's improvement and literary societies connected with
the Church ; there was even a small laboratory at home
that he and his brother used for chemical experiments
when they were home from college.   The other went
to a shipbroker's office.   He was a little later of getting
home, he was a little dirtier when he got home, but he
had a larger salary.   By the time he had dined, and
dressed up, he had money enough to enjoy himself
without study.   He went into town to meet his office
companions, a ship captain occasionally, who treated
the boys liberally.   They visited, now a music-hall, now
a billiard saloon, now no higher than a friendly public
house.   It was a sad blow to his father and his brother,
that this young man should have given up, as they
said, the pure joys of intellectual occupations and become
so worldly.   The young fellow felt bad about it himself,
not knowing the true reason, and being brought up in
that agreeable faith, that you are to blame the devil
for everything you do not understand, should it turn
out bad.   All he knew was that study now was distasteful, and his mind ran on other pleasures.   The
parson sought many reasons to account for the disparity
of tastes between his two sons, and he found as
many as he sought, some hereditary, some consti-
tutional, some profoundly psychical.   He consoled
himself with the reflection and assurance that at least
one of his children loved wisdom for its own sake, and

delighted in the pursuit of knowledge. Alas! poor
man ; he went and destroyed that happy consolation
himself. He had occasionally to look at the worldly
side of things, and when he did so, as regards the
welfare of his children, he had some thoughts at the
inequality of their future. The shipbroking youth was
pushing himself on rapidly, and would soon have a free
expenditure as great as his father's, while his studious
brother was still keeping his clothes clean on an annual
increment of five pounds. It was enough for merely
recording discounts and overdrafts, but it was likely to
be a long time before it would be enough to live upon.
The parson spoke to some friends, and the young man
was transferred to a merchant's warehouse. In a little
time also came the transformation. Like his brother,
this studious young man began to come home late, and
in a great hurry ; wanted dinner in haste ; had no time
to speak to any body ; was going to meet his companions
at such a time, and was likely to be late ; they were all
going to see something or another, and he might be late
of getting home ; there would be no use of any body
sitting up for him. This was the chronic state of
affairs : wild horses could not get this studious
youth to spend an evening at home, or to take an
interest in his old pursuits. He was making money
now.

The manufacturing town or the seaport town may,
and often do, have as many young men of liberal
education, sons of wealthy manufacturers or ship-
owners, as the town, noted as the centre of banking,
insurance, or financial institutions, but they never have
the same intellectual tone. They are always more interested in current events, because they can afford to
keep themselves abreast of current events. The manufacturing or seaport town, though not large, will have
a theatre, music-halls, and all the recognised places

of public amusement, and these will be well patronised.
The banking town, though larger, may have a theatre,
which is not well patronised. There is but one audience,
and it cannot go more than once a week to the theatre
It therefore does not go for pleasure, but for instruction,
and like a lecture, or a sermon, a week is little enough
for the drama's thorough discussion and digestion.

If religion or education could be made of service by
the Poor in their daily struggle with straitened means
although the one is to them unduly repressive at the time
they most enjoy their freedom, and the other requires a
vacant mind and large allowance of leisure—even in the
face of these difficulties they would make a bold effort to
attain them. But they cannot see the merit in these
things themselves, nor can they see around them any
example of people who have cultivated the one or the
other as a cure for poverty.

As a sample of how the intellectual and the unintel-
lectual, applied to the same thing, affect the Poor, we
will take the following :

In the poorer districts of every large town there have
been for years mission churches, mission halls, and
mission stations. Some districts are perfectly honey-
combed with them. To those who are not used to
mission work, we may state, briefly, these halls are
miniature churches, open on certain days in the week
for the propagation of religion in the neighbourhood.
The audience at the most successful of them leaves
much to be desired ; the general average is two or
three benches of steady old retainers. Sometimes "to
brighten up the service a bit," or "to make it more
interesting," they have the assistance of a fashionable
parson or popular lecturer. A young lady presides at
the harmonium, and a choir of young ladies and young
gentlemen in many instances give their services to
render the music. Everything is done that can be done

to attract the people from the streets, but they refuse to be drawn.

Into this district of over-supplied and empty mission houses marches the Salvation Army. We are speaking of it in its early days, its days of phenomenal successes in the face of every obstacle that prejudice and jealousy could raise against it. Here there were neither reverence nor repression, all was excitement and employment. Every person could join in and take a hand, all the work was done by themselves. They sang their own hymns, and made them to suit their taste. They fitted them with stolen music from the "Halls," and they replaced the intellectual harmonium with the brainless drum and untutored cymbals. They had other musical instruments which they could not play very well, but everybody's own noise is music, it is other people's music that is noise. They were content with the noise they made with their instruments, and so were the majority of their hearers. The instruments were there less for their sweet strains than that they were excellent mediums for the players to exhibit their enthusiasm and earnestness. Everything that could exhilarate, excite, and inspire enthusiasm was incorporated into their service. The enthusiasm of the performers was contagious, and the listener felt, no matter what his abilities or his ambitions were, there was room for the development of them all in the ranks of the "Army."

To the Poor the Army was less a religion than an agreeable occupation. Unlike the mission hall, that only opened on special nights, they could engage themselves in salvation work every night, as long as the excitement, the strangeness, and the enthusiasm lasted. All the terms of their service were adapted to take the mind from reverence and reverend associations, and to cultivate their natural pugnacious instincts. They hated the name of religion, and they suspected any

person who attempted to coax them to come and
hear this man speak, or such a choir sing. Whatever
suggested a hall and the necessity of sitting quiet for
half an hour or an hour, they knew would be accompanied with the certain prayer and praise and exhorta-
tion. But ask them to come and storm hell or make a
grand assault upon the devil, or have some knee drill,
or whatever terms they used, and it appeared to them
quite a different thing.

Between the Salvation Army realism—vulgarism if
you will—and the Higher Criticism, the Inner Holiness,
the Symbolism and the Mysticism, that the D.D.'s
M.A.'s, Fellows of Colleges, and other highly intellectual
churchmen delight to dabble in, there does not seem to
be anything in common but the name Religion. Yet
the devotee of the one would not change it for the other,
and the Poor would have remained to this day without
any religion rather than accept the intellectual kind so
long offered them, and offered them in vain.

When the writer, full of strong religious convictions,
found it was impossible to be of service to the Poor
unless through the laws that governed their lives—
Natural law—he met with a great disappointment ; one
he, for the time being, believed would prove fatal.
There was nothing he had been taught from his youth
up more emphatically and persistently than that all our
evil actions arose from our natural inclinations ; that
our natures were inherently evil, and required repression
and discipline, and that anything suggestive of Nature
as a sole guide to action was at once denounced, and
compared to the lives of the brutes in the fields ; that
all that Nature taught us was to eat, to drink, and care
nothing for to-morrow, because to-morrow was not
ours. Was it then to propagate vice and passion that
we had stirred ourselves so ? And if nothing but evil
was to come of our attempts to help the Poor from their

distress, was it not better they should be left to perish,
and perish quickly, that the tale of guilt would be so
much the less ?

But the writer knew the Poor, had known them all
his life, and he knew they were not going to change
their habits because he believed he had made a discovery ! They were, in fact, quite ignorant that he had
made such a discovery, and if he had informed them,
they would have ignored the information and gone on
their way as usual. To the writer, however, despair
gave way to hope. This then, said he, is Natural law ;
there is no bestiality here ; there is no straining after
vice ; there is no lack of hope, ambition, or desire
for improvement. What overlies these virtues in
the Poor is the pressing demands of their necessities. Their bodies are ever in need—one thing or
another—and the body is the natural master of
the mind. When we studied each life individually,
even the very worst of them, they had a natural
virtuous bent. They would rather do a good turn
than a bad one.

The study of Natural law was necessary then, to see
where the Poor differed in their actions from the other
classes : whether the cause of that difference lay in themselves, or in circumstances outside of themselves ; and
in either case, what was the origin of these causes.
After years of study and experiment, we came to the
conclusion that the difference between the Poor and the
Rich so far as law-breaking is concerned, lies mostly in
their social condition. The cultivation by groups of
people of special forms of life, habits, and customs, to
the extent as to make other forms intolerable to them,
and therefore, where they have the power, to attempt
the suppression of such forms is one of the most prolific
causes of the Poor offending. The Poor do not make
their own amusements, their habits, fashions, or cus-

toms; all these have descended to them from the better classes of a past age. But unfortunately, these pleasures only reach the Poor when the better classes of the present age have condemned them, and legislated against them because the Poor refuse to give them up voluntarily. Yet the better classes of the past who introduced these condemned manners would not have surrendered them to the Poor of their day, or the wise, or any class even at the threat of a revolution, but praised them, clung to them, extolled them, and left a long catalogue of plays, romances, poems, and songs in their glorification. Their descendants, the better classes of the present day, are following in their footsteps as regards the pleasures of the hour, and their grand- or great-grand- children will be busy legislating against these pleasures just as the Poor of their time have succeeded to them.

The Social Life is our true formative life; it is our only free life wherein our natural desires show their course and inclination, form the habits most suitable to them, and utilise all the conditions of our life in their own service. Our business has its conditions, so also has our rest. There must be a wide difference then between the enjoyment of a life, from which all obstacles are removed by legislation, and the enjoyment of a life that as much legislation as can reasonably be passed is made to hamper and forbid. These are the different conditions of life under which wealth and poverty exist. There is no legislation interferes with the pleasures of the Rich; there is hardly a pleasure of the Poor that is not under some form of restriction. This burden of repression—brain repression—becomes to all men at certain times intolerable, but more especially at a time of pleasure. Almost our first action of enjoyment is mental and physical freedom, the relieving all our muscles, nerves, and limbs, and thoughts from their usual restraint. The Rich have no restraint to throw off when they wish to enjoy themselves. They do so every day, and it is the habit of their lives ; but the Poor cannot enjoy themselves without throwing off restraint, and to do so is generally a police offence.

It may be wondered by some why, as the Poor change their habits, they cannot be persuaded to make a great step forward and at once adopt the habits of the wealthy classes of their own time, and so live in their approval and concurrent morality. Such a question looks superfluous on paper, yet it is asked every day in the actions of those philanthropists and missionaries who preach to the Poor on their evil ways. The Poor as well as the Rich adopt their habits by Natural law, and are no more responsible for them than a lady is for the fashion she will wear next year ; and the philanthropist who disapproves of the habits of the Poor and approves of his own, is as unaware why he is addicted to the habits of his life as he is why golf became fashionable. Social habits are adopted by the law of Imitation, one of the strongest laws in humanity ; but our freedom of imitation is restricted by the social law of Uniformity, and we can only adopt as a habit what our own set agree upon adopting.

We have touched upon this one instance of how the Rich make the lives of the Poor unnecessarily difficult to them by their intolerance. Each class of society is following a natural law in the formation of circles of uniformity, but here Nature ceases ; it is civilisation, and especially religion that teaches us to condemn all other formations but our own. Nature has ordained that we shall each of us form the individual and social habits and customs in which we find life easiest and can pursue our happiness with least hindrance ; but it stops at interfering with the owners of other lives doing the same. But civilisation, education, or religion (we mention all three so that each reader may choose for himself which he believes to be the true formative force within us) has brought us to a pass that it seems the only happiness left to one half of the world, is to forbid the other to have any. When these earnest people come to know some day, as it is to be hoped they will, that virtue springs naturally from happiness, they may reflect upon the amount they are treading out of existence each year in their efforts to propagate it.

The definition of Natural law or the laws of Nature in life are very diverse and vague. It depends largely on education and prejudice. To some people it is the mechanical satisfaction of the physical necessities. They exclude the use of the intelligences. Like the animals, they say, when a man is hungry, he takes the first loaf he sees, no matter whose it may be, and he eats it. And further, as long as there is eatable matter to be had, this man will remain as he is, and eat when he is hungry. To such people Natural law is an insufficient guide to existence. It means stagnation and animalism. Others again admit in Natural law the use of the intellectual faculties, but only for the purpose of showing, that it only uses them on the immoral side —never for a virtuous purpose. This is the opinion of the pietists. The heart of man, they say, is deceitful and desperately wicked. It is to be continually watched over, and its desires repressed.

Self-preservation is the first law of Nature, it is said. If a person fell into the water, would he not try and save himself, and in so doing would he not use all his brains and experience? Then would this be an immoral because natural use of one's intelligence? A learned professor[1] has just said in a lecture :—"Then, again,

[1] Prof. William Wallace, of Oxford. Fifth of the Glasgow Gifford Lectures, season 1894-95. As reported in *Glasgow Herald*, March 1, 1895.

the modern [critics] said the natural was immoral.
What a ghastly prospect was set forth in that statement. We could not abjure Nature. In ninety-nine
hundredths of our life we must be natural. Were we
therefore immoral?"

In the opinion of the writer, Natural laws, or the laws
of Nature, are the uniform, inalienable conditions to
which all life is born, and through which alone it can
attain happiness. Were the universe stationary, and the
environment of life always the same, these laws would act
without deviation or variation, and life everywhere would
be mechanical and automatic. In such a case life would
require no brains, having no choice of action. But
because all the world is changing and unforseeable,
even we ourselves, Nature has supplied life with a
faculty to surmount, or at least contend with, the difficulty. This common faculty we, in ourselves, call
Reason, and are very proud of the extent to which we
are endowed with it over other forms of life. The
original use of brains and their equivalent in other
forms of life is only that of selection. We hunger and
we thirst every day, and several times a day; yet we
never hunger or thirst under exactly the same conditions, either as regards ourselves or our means of
satisfying them. Even when the same means are at
hand, they must take their chance with all other means
available. It is the function of the brain to satisfy
this ever-changing desire; and it is a question of
education and prejudice why we differ so widely in
doing so. The professor, the bishop, and the working
man may all thirst at the same time, and the one will
assuage himself with water, another with wine, and
the third with beer, and each will prefer his own
method, and in doing so is following a natural law.
While Natural law is careful over the twitching of a
muscle, or the bending of a finger, there is also room

within its scope for the grandest, the wildest, the most delicate or most profound thought the brain is capable of. Our thoughts lie to our point of strongest desire as the needle to the pole. The banker thinks of money-making, and the lover of his mistress ; the poet of his rhymes, and the soldier of ambition. But all of them have at times strong desires, to which their thoughts lie close, but which they carefully guard against publicity. The strongest desires of the Poor are always physical comfort and rest. Life itself would have to be destroyed before that could be altered.

The subject and classification of Natural laws is too vast for discussion here. Our apology for touching upon it at all, is that many of these laws are referred to throughout the following pages, and it would be a fair reproach of the reader's against us, that we have introduced new or contentious matter without putting the whole argument from which we draw our deductions before them. Until a future day, we are afraid that reproach must lie against us, but in the meantime we hope that with the definition of Natural law we have just given, and the explanation of each we have made in referring to it, the reader will be able to understand our meaning, though he may dispute our conclusions.

To the Poor Law systems of the country we make no reference : they are outside the scope of our argument. A legal enactment is not a philanthropy, and it is with philanthropy alone we propose to deal in the meantime —whether the voluntary interference of one class with the lives of another class is for the good of that other class or not ? The question is put as boldly as can be. It is admitted that the interfering class believe they are intermeddling for the other's good ; but this is denied by the Poor, unless in the one particular of the free-gift-to-all-comers' mission. It is admissible that we

C 2

should incorporate into the simple question we have set before us, the further one—whether it is morally and economically just that a class or section of the community should supply, free of cost, to another section of the community those things that Nature and a healthy state of society require they should work to provide for themselves?

CHAPTER II

Philanthropy: its subjection to moral law—The different moral laws of the different classes—Class a barrier to sympathy—Natural philanthropy and unnatural philanthropies.

WHAT is philanthropy? The word means "love of mankind," and a philanthropist is a person who loves his fellow man and fellow men. It is a compound of two Greek words meant to embody the idea of universal brotherhood. As regards real life no such thing or person ever existed, or could exist.

In the opinion of many, these ideal conceptions of life, though known to be impossible of attainment, are looked upon as serving a good purpose in encouraging people—mostly young—to strive to attain as near as possible to them, so that in the effort they may reach a higher possible standard than has yet been attained. The common advice to the young is, "to always keep before you a high ideal, always strive to reach it or as near to it as you can." This would be very good advice, if and where the limit of human action is unknown, but where the limit of our efforts is perfectly well known these impossible ideals, in the experience of the writer, do more harm than good. They often deprive the person of all inclination to make any effort, because they are known beforehand to be unattainable. And they are quoted as justifications for making no special effort, by the lazy and unambitious, who say that it is no use trying impossibilities.

The impossibility of any person loving the whole human family, or even all of that infinitesimal portion he personally comes in contact with, lies in this, that he would have to be a person without any knowledge of good or evil. According to Natural law—not civilisation's laws—not even a lunatic is without that knowledge, and therefore without likes and dislikes.

The origin of good and evil springs from our personal experience. Our object in life—the object of each individual—is to find his happiness, and in pursuit of that object we love—nor can help ourselves—all who assist us, and are friendly to us ; and we hate all who would hinder us or are wilfully antagonistic to us, nor can we help that hate. That is the primary moral law of all men, and remains throughout life the strongest.

Civilisation made in each country, and according to the social habits of the people, and to a certain extent in accordance with its religion, a common uniform code of morality to supersede our personal and individual ones. And so comes our national sense of right and wrong.

The moral code, or code of right and wrong that obtains among the people with whom we have to deal and amidst whom our life is cast, is the code we generally accept for our own guidance. It is the easiest to live, the one we can depend upon as guiding the actions of others towards ourselves, and we can no more love the person who wilfully violates it, and so hurts the community, and ourselves as part of it, than we can love the person who turns us to ridicule. Our

actions generally, or at least our free actions, we must
believe to be right, seeing they are the result of our
own reasoning. The person who seeks to turn them to
ridicule, by so doing seeks to persuade others that they
are wrong. We cannot love the person who seeks to
make us wrong when we believe we are right.

No man can love what he believes to be wrong, and
to love the person who is guilty of the wrong is to love
the wrong itself.

The highest human nature can attain to in dealing with
the wrong : we can suspend our resentment of it : we
can forgive : we can pity—but we cannot love. To do
so were to cross the barrier and approve of it.

Wherever the community is divided into classes
there is another barrier raised to our efforts at philanthropy, in its Greek sense. The sympathy of the
classes flows upwards and not downwards, in the very
opposite direction to our desire to help. We cannot
love the class below our own : we tolerate them. They
are the heirs to our cast-off habits, as we are the
successors to the habits of the class immediately above
us. It may have been a generation or two ago since we
discarded the habits that are fashionable with our lower
class. Having disused them we also condemned them,
and we can entertain no warm affection for the class
that continues them. As with the class immediately
next to our own, so is it with all the classes below us
down to the bottom, increasing in degree as we descend,
because the habits they affect are older, longer in time
given up by us, and thought therefore more disreputable.
It is the penalty we pay for social life that our
sympathies and affections seldom descend below our
own class.

The writer experienced an ecstasy of love for the Poor
that lasted about five years. So strong was the passion
upon him that he felt it no effort to be capable of any

sacrifice for them. To be of service to them he spent
all his leisure with them. He became one of themselves
as far as he could ; he suppressed all social distinction
not to offend them ; he determined to see no evil in
their actions where they saw none, not to rouse their
prejudice. What he disapproved of he remained silent
upon, not to lose their confidence. He went among
them denuded of every feeling but that of wishing to
help them. He drank with them, so far as he could
drink, to find out whether drink was to them a necessity or an indulgence. He had only two ambitions—to
promote their happiness, and to solve, if possible, the
mystery—if mystery there were—of their lives ; whether
they were living the highest form of virtue their
circumstances permitted, or whether, according to
every missionary's story and police report, they de-
liberately preferred evil to good. These two ambitions
worked on entirely different lines, and produced in the
writer a strange consciousness of a double existence.
The enthusiastic one had no thought for anything but
how to make the poor he met with happy ; how for the
time he was with them he could give them some
pleasure, remove from them some annoyance, settle as
far as he could that they should not suffer for a little in
advance. He cared not what the cost, if he could do
it ; was oblivious to all after-effects of his actions.
Sufficient for the day was its own misery ; if that could
be lifted, we could hope for the morrow. But there
was no day looked upon as satisfactorily spent that had
not made some happy faces, brightened some home, or
relieved some despondency ; and the night only brought
a prayer for greater strength, and dreams of further
usefulness.

The observant side of our existence was unimpas-
sioned, cool, and collected, observing everything, re-
membering everything, watching faces and actions,

permitting no detail, however trifling, to escape. It tried
to see behind the grimy veil of hardened and expressionless muscles ; it sought to penetrate beyond the
bleary film of the eye. What was going on in the
brain, what the impelling and repressive forces at work
upon the intelligence ; these were the observations and
reflections of this side of our work. And at night, when
at home, everything was weighed and summed up ;
probable motives were imagined, to be tested next
opportunity ; effects were calculated upon, to be watched
and followed to their conclusion.

This dual existence, strange though it seems, worked
perfectly harmoniously. The enthusiastic impulse was
immensely the stronger and felt no restraint ; the other
side was simply observant. It made no protest, but
summed up its conclusions every night and presented
them to the working side as a kind of guide to the
morrow's work.

But the strangest thing of all was that after some
time the observant side began to close its nightly
reflections with the remark, "You do not love the
Poor!" For some time this remark passed unheeded.
It was so preposterous! To feel one's self sometimes
vibrating with this emotion ; to have no thought night
nor day but how to serve them, and yet to be told we
did not love the Poor. What could be the motive of
our actions ? We worked alone, and spoke to no person
about our doings but those personal friends who knew
what we were doing. We felt safer to trust our own
feelings in the matter, than heed our other self's over
cautious speculations. Besides, it would not have
mattered, we could not help ourself. But the nightly
repetition of the remark had the same effect as
the drop of water upon the stone. It wore a place for
itself into our thoughts, that we found it getting daily
more difficult to ignore. We found ourself thinking

of it when we had imagined we had banished it. We
found it coming between us and our work. It must
therefore be faced and satisfactorily settled. Something
like the following conversation took place between our
dual self. " Why do you say I do not love the Poor ? "
" Because in fact you do not do so." " Knowing the
feelings that possess us, and the way we spend our
time, what other motive or incentive could we have ? "
" You do not act towards the Poor as you do to
people you love, not even as to people of your own
class with whom you are only intimate." " Have I not
suppressed all class distinction ? Do I not make them
my equals in all things, speak to them and act to them
as one of themselves ; have I not overcome my prejudices against their ways and doings ? " " Yes, in
outward appearance, but not in feeling. Your feelings
remain in their natural state, and you have to exercise
an effort of will to overcome them. Nor is one effort
enough ; each night you have to renew it, sometimes
more than once in a night. With the people you like,
you require to suppress nothing ; no effort is required
to spend the time with them, nor is your mind even
occupied with the subject." " That may arise from
long habit and education. The people of my own class
I understand better and our thoughts flow more freely ;
also we have the same moral code, the same principle,
the same ideas of right and wrong." " But the difference in your feeling does not arise from these causes,
because it is not confined to your own class, nor your
own principles. When you spent your holiday at that
little fishing village last summer you took a liking to
the natives. There was the very drunken butcher, who
sometimes fell off his cart. You felt no inclination to
condemn his conduct ; you only laughed at his help-
lessness. There was the very blasphemous boatman !
the choleric old fisherman. You felt no prejudice

against their faults ; you good-naturedly overlooked all
their faults because you liked them, and yet your principles were opposed to their lives.   But it is not so with
the Poor.   If one gives way to swearing, you do not
laugh ; you become grave, but say nothing.   If you find
one of your poor acquaintances tipsy, you do not enjoy
the joke.   You have to stay with him and see him
home.   Should one get into a passion and be inclined
to fight, it is not the funny thing it was in the
summer, but a very serious matter.   When you like
one set of Poor whose habits you disapprove of, why do
you not treat the other set the same ? "   " I was not
thinking of the Poor of the village to interest myself in
them, and to help them."   " The greater the interest
the greater the affection.   It should make you all the
more able to forgive the city Poor ; yet you know such
is not the case."   Silence for a few minutes.   Again
the enthusiast : " What then can be this impelling
motive within me, over which I have so little command,
if it is not love ? "   " It *is* love, but not of the Poor.   Not
of any one of them, not of the whole regiment.   It is
love of their well-being, their happiness.   Intense
study of their condition—what you called the ' Question
of the Poor '—brought you an idea that you could solve
the problem of their happiness.   The constant contemplation of the immense benefit to civilisation, let alone
the Poor, you would confer, if successful, kept your
mind in a frenzy, and the gorgeous pictures, the realisa-
tion of your hopes, kept passing panorama-wise before
your mind supplied the daily stimulant."   " With all
that, taking you at your own words, how can I love the
welfare and happiness of the Poor yet not love the
Poor ? "   " Easily enough ; it is your idea of their
happiness you love, not them.   All of them who happen
to walk with you on that line you can love readily
enough ; but they are very few, the great majority are

going their own way, crossing and recrossing your
track, sometimes obstructing it, and these you cannot
love. You cannot love two opposite principles at one
and the same time ; you cannot love their happiness
and those of them that hinder and thwart it."

Such is the case with all philanthropists : they are fully
persuaded that they love the Poor ; but the philanthropist may be better described as, not one who loves the
Poor, but one who hates their ways. A man who loves
the Poor must love them as they are, and therefore
would not seek to change them. A man who is contented with the lives of his fellow men is never a
philanthropist. In philanthropy we must first see
something we dislike. How then can we love those
that continue against our efforts in the objectionable
state ? This is the state of civilised philanthropy where
the different classes lead different lives. Were we all
of one class this form of philanthropy could not exist ;
as nobody objects to the habits of his own class,
nobody was ever known to missionise his own set.

As Nature made no arrangement for people to live in
strata, Natural philanthropy is of a different form. It
is purely individual, as Nature meant all life to be, and
it is neither a philosophical nor divine conception. It
is purely self-defensive—the strongest spur to action
that we have.

Pain is the great arch-enemy of that happiness we
are all bound to seek. We cannot endure it ourselves ;
all our faculties are trained to watch for it and avoid
it, and to relieve ourselves of it when it comes to us.
We cannot even endure the sight or the knowledge of
it in others. That Natural philanthropy is no virtue
is evidenced in this— it is not the other person's pain we
relieve by our philanthropical efforts, but our own.
The person through whom we are made to suffer may
be able to bear with equanimity what is acute distress

to us, yet that does not arrest our efforts to have it
removed.   From this fact arises the folly of many
missions.   The Poor have greater power of endurance
than the higher classes, yet the higher classes start
missions among the Poor to relieve them of what by
the standard of endurance of the better classes must be
great misery, but by the standard of the Poor is hardly
more than a passing inconvenience.

Natural philanthropy cannot be systematised.   It
must wait the incident and occasion that calls it forth,
and it can go no further than the satisfactory settlement
of that case, until it is awakened again by some new
circumstance.   It is simplicity itself, as perfect in the
helping of an old lady over a crossing, or picking
up an old gentleman who has fallen, as in feeding
thousands in a famine-stricken country.   It never errs,
and can never be improved upon, for, like all Nature's
laws, it works perfectly, and has no exception.

It is upon this Natural law of suffering that social
philanthropy is founded.   It does not look much the
same thing, and those who affect social philanthropy
prefer putting it upon a higher plane—sometimes
spiritual, sometimes sentimental.   The comparison
between them is only this—where they differ social
philanthropy goes wrong.   The social philanthropist
must first feel a distress before he is roused to action,
but instead of relieving, or helping to relieve the distress
he feels, he must generalise that all that class, or all
that particular neighbourhood where it was exhibited
suffer alike, and from the same cause.   The districts
where the Poor live are so congested, that it is safe to
say, within the same area they stand to the wealthy
quarters in population as ten to one.   When a West
End lady sees a little boy standing at one of the entries
in a poor quarter, bootless, and apparently cold, she is
moved by her own suffering at the sight.   So far, quite

natural. But she takes for granted that all the children in the neighbourhood are starving with cold because of their bootless condition, and through the press and the platform she makes piteous appeals for funds to start a mission to clothe " the little ones," especially their pedal extremities. So far she is as reasonable as if the father of that boy visited the West End, and came to the conclusion that all the men of that district required their hair cut because he saw a minor poet walking down Regent Street.

Unfortunate also, is it, that social philanthropy should be based on the same principle of personal suffering as Natural philanthropy, because it is those possessed of least endurance who are the leading philanthropists—the hysterical, the neurotic, the fibre- less. They are the first to scream out at anything they fear may be disagreeable to them, and they call their selfishness by such fine names as " Refined Sensi- bilities," " Public Morality," "Common Humanity." We have called them selfish, but they do not think they are selfish, and the word may sound too harsh. But the action is selfish all the same. In their opinion everything is due to them from the public ; nothing is due from them to the public. The murderer must escape the law because *they* do not like capital punish- ment. The judge's decision must be overturned, and the law of the country brought into contempt, because *they* dislike its penalties. Thieves and false accusers must escape scot-free, because there are circumstances in their career that are interesting. They care nothing for the protection of life or property, regard for the law, or social customs, when their sensibilities are affected. Public opinion or State policy must surrender to them at once before their sufferings can be assuaged. And what do they render in return ? Let State necessity or local requirements but touch some of their many prejudices, and then listen to the howl! Not though hundreds of young men go to an early grave each year from preventible causes would they yield one iota of their selfish requirements. These are the extreme ; but they will soon be the only philanthropists. All others they are driving from the field. To be moderate or sensible is—in their eyes—to differ from them, and that is a greater crime than breaking the whole moral law. They are the extremists for weakness at one end of the social ladder, and the Poor are the extremists for hardihood at the other ; and when they take to interesting themselves in the affairs of the Poor, the Poor smile, and rather like it.

The rational philanthropist is in no way more removed from being governed by his feelings than the Natural one. He may take an immensely wider view of the problem of life, but there had first to be a sore that vexed him before he took any view at all. He may pass by the sores, or wounds, seeing in them only evidences of a deep-seated, malignant disease that threatens a fatal development. He may consider it no case for local treatment, and give his mind to a remedial and general course of treatment. But it is the surface wound that shows the disease, and according to its painful effect upon us is the interest and activity we show in its removal.

There is no man can err in helping the removal of the distress he may see in his daily round, unless by giving money. Money is seldom required ; but our faith in its power to be a substitute for everything, and our cowardice in the face of trouble, makes us ever ready to buy ourselves off from a disagreeable duty. By so doing we have created a nice, large class who prey upon the public sympathy—from the man who, with a piece of soap in his mouth, can simulate fits, to the comfortable and cosy begging-letter writers who make their five and ten pounds a week. These people when found out we punish; yet it is we who have created them. An epileptic person requires no money, but a physician; and if that plan were followed he would cease to be epileptic. A begging-letter is seldom written to a person residing in the same town as the writer thereof, or where the case, so pathetically and distressingly described, is supposed to occur. No person should send money to any one not in his own town. Each town has enough, and more than enough, philanthropists to take charge of its own distress. Exceptional cases of affliction such as the begging-letter writer loves to portray cannot be hidden, and must be known locally, and are sure of being treated.

With the exception of these pests, our practice of Natural philanthropy is free from being imposed upon. None can tell our pain endurance, and if it be a case we do not feel causes or entails much suffering, our sympathies are not aroused. Should they be aroused, we only require to help the sufferer to relief from his suffering, we do not require to buy for him immunity —that is no philanthropy. But there is one thing about Natural philanthropy different from all the other systems : it requires to respect no moral or ethical code. We cannot justify many of the causes of our own sufferings; as a rule we seldom can morally defend any of them; but all the same we are diligent in seeking relief from them. So also must it be with our sympathetic pain; we require to ask no questions how it came there, we have only to remove it. Nature has protected us from the repetition of any action where the sufferer may think to profit by our sympathy—the sympathy passes into indifference. Note how our sympathies are aroused at the sight of a new form of distress; but after we have seen it every day for a month or two, note our indifference.

It is claimed by those whose opinion we are entitled to respect, that Natural philanthropy is not sufficient to meet the difficulties in a large town. We answer, that it has never been tried ; and that in our own experience the cases of real distress requiring aid are very few. There are plenty *evidences* of distress, some the natural condition of the people, and some short acute forms that are known not to be of any duration, and for which the sufferers do nothing themselves, and that would be gone and forgotten before one could arrange to do anything. But the distress that is unusual, and likely to last for a time, and beyond the effort of the sufferers themselves to contend with, is very much rarer than is generally understood. We cannot say, ourselves, whether individual philanthropy would be adequate to cope with all the legitimate distress in a very congested district, calculating all the people of the better classes who may have occasion to find their way there, but we advocate it to all and sundry as the only form of philanthropy that can do neither themselves nor the poor any harm ; in fact, do both much good. The time is coming, and coming faster than many people think, when the socialistic demands of the Poor, to which our legislators are helplessly sinking, will arouse the classes to an indignant sense of self-defence, and all philanthropy will cease on the ground that it is no longer necessary to help those who have learned so well how to help themselves. A sense of ingratitude and injustice will strengthen all against any flow of sympathy, no matter what the apparent distress. At that time it may be serviceable to the reader to know of a system of philanthropy that can be exercised without hurt to any one.

However, we must consider things as they are, and not as they should be, if we wish to make any practical progress. As long as the classes in large towns love each other so indifferently that they prefer living in

different quarters—the rich always furthest away from
the poor—some artificial form of philanthropy may be
necessary. And as long as we believe that all the inhabitants of a poor district are synchronically starving,
synchronically drunk, and uniformly irreligious, there
may be some reason for systematising our philanthropical efforts on a permanent, continuous basis.
Few people believe all the Poor to be one thing or
another at the same time, but we always speak at our
missions and write of them as if there dwelt no
exception among them. It is always the great misery
and starvation *of* the Poor—not among them ; the
awful intemperance *of* the Poor ; the fearful impiety *of*
the Poor.

An organised philanthropy in which more than one
person is concerned must of course have a principle.
It is the binding element of subscribers, managers,
and organisers, and no matter what that principle may
be, if it is a moral one, dealing with a line of conduct—
one we should all like to see the Poor adopt for their own
sakes—then *there* ends the mission's usefulness at once.
The Poor have their own moral code ; it is not ours.
We cannot adopt theirs ; they cannot adopt ours. This
question of morality separates the classes more than
anything next to wealth, but it destroys the sympathy
between the classes more than wealth does.

A digression here to explain our meaning may be
permitted. By morality or moral law we do not mean
the decalogue. That instrument, we take it, was a
hurried declaration of the two great principles of
government that had existed for all time in savage as
well as in civilised peoples ; the two principles by which
any form of order alone can exist. The first five an-
nouncements establish authority from that of God to
the parent ; and the last five, the protection of property
from that of life and wife down to reputation.

National morality, as we have said at the beginning of this chapter, is a guide to our actions one to another as citizens of the same country. It is based on the spirit of existing laws ; an extension of their principles beyond the limit where penalties can be enforced. But though people of the same nation, we are mostly strangers to each other, and our intercourse in many cases is very limited ; and so national morality is an insufficient guide to our conduct. Each separate act should have its ethical principle understood by the doer, the sufferer, and the witnesses. Social life is the fullest life we have, and the morality that springs therefrom is generally the governing laws of our conduct. The social habits of each class are different, and therefore so must their morality be. Each approve of their own habitual actions, and their perceptions of good and evil are modelled and educated upon these actions. That hardly any one class can approve wholly of the actions of another class shows they have a different morality. They all live under the same laws, and the preponderating majority have had the same fundamental education in religion. It is not these that influence and guide our lives most, but the morality of our class. It modifies our interpretation of both religion and law.

The difference, then, of educational from Natural philanthropy is the moral note introduced into the former, and that is also its stumbling block. This has been recognised for some years past by certain philanthropists, and they have established relieving missions free from the educational taint. In most of the large towns in the country there are missions for feeding, clothing, sheltering, and otherwise providing the Poor with anything they stand in need of—free, gratis, and for nothing, not even a hymn being required of them. But still these missions cannot wholly do without the moral safeguard. Like all missions, it is other people's

money the managers are working upon, and before
they can find people willing to part with their money,
the subscribers require a guarantee that the money
must be used for a good purpose. The guarantee that
is forthcoming is that all cases are specially inquired
into before help is given. Any one acquainted with the
ways of the Poor will know of what value such a
guarantee is. It is one of the highest moral principles
of a large worthless class to swindle both mission and
missionary, because of the total lack of sympathy
between them, and of the contempt the Poor have for
the stupid way the philanthropist goes about his work.
While the distributing mission is advertising for funds,
it seems to forget that it is also advertising to all and
sundry among the Poor where to get food and clothing
for the asking—always in a proper manner. There are
a great many among the Poor to whom a great-coat,
or a pair of boots, or even a good square meal comes
in handy at any time, and although they may not have
been thinking about them at any particular time, the
advertisement where to go reminds them not to lose the
opportunity. That they can satisfy the special inquiry
they have no fear; they live all the year round and
enjoy a life that would bring tears to the eyes of the
tender-hearted, well-fed, well-clothed philanthropists
who " run " the mission. But should they suspect they
are not down to the necessary requirements all they
require to do is to strip in a neighbouring entry to the
proper nakedness, and give their pal their clothes to
hold until they come back. The variation from Natural
philanthropy that the distributing philanthropy shows,
is, that instead of relieving the distress that has
occurred the latter advertises to the Poor that a certain
evidence of distress, accompanied by the ability to
stand a certain inspection, entitles all to relief gratis.
Now if there is any class among the Poor whose lives

always show these evidences they are not in distress, yet they are eligible for relief. There is such a class, and these missions are their great propagating agencies.

The interfering with the normal conditions of any person's life is not philanthropy.

The intermittent thrusting of pleasures upon the Poor—pleasures they cannot indulge in themselves—is not philanthropy.

The artificial augmentation of their earning power or spending power is no philanthropy.

And, above all, the attempts of a weaker class to gauge what is the suffering of a strong class destroys in both that fortitude which is the sole hope for the regeneration of mankind.

CHAPTER III

The Church's influence on philanthropy, showing the evolution of
public charity from the Church as first almoner to the
mission becoming more important than the Poor.

THERE is no such thing in Nature as a free gift, or as
it may more familiarly be described, Nature's law is
"nothing for nothing." Nature has made no provision
how one man's possessions can become another person's
without an equivalent. What we call free gifts are only
gifts to which we do not attach conditions for repayment
that can be legally enforced. But that they are not free is
proved by the fact that they create new and different relations between the giver and the receiver, from that
in which they stood before. These new relations in the
minds of both are a credit of obligation on the one side, a
debit of obligation on the other. The obligation represents the equivalent of the gift, but is left blank.

If there were such a thing as a free gift, the relationship of the parties towards each other would remain
unchanged, a manifest impossibility. Should a person
find some money, he is personally the gainer by the
amount found, but his relations to his fellow men remain
unaltered by the find. But should he receive it as a

free gift from any one ; while all the rest remain the same, his relations to that one person are changed by reason of the gift.

The workings of this Natural law will be seen in the Church's relations to philanthropy.

The Church was the first organised professional almoner.   There were many circumstances in past history why it should be so.   It was for many turbulent years the only stable permanent institution of civilisation.   The history of the toilers—all who are condemned to earn their bread by the sweat of their brow—can be written in three short chapters from the date of civilisation :—Slavery—with the minimum of poverty and no philanthropy.   Feudalism—whereby the peasant was allowed to work for himself when his master did not require him—a fee for his land in peace time, and bodily service in war.   Emancipation—when the fee was increased to cover all obligations.

Feudalism caused many Poor—the widows and children of those slain in battle, and the wounded, maimed, and incapacitated, who could no longer work. There was an obligation upon the superior—Lord or Chieftain—to support these people, and to whom could that duty be delegated when the clan was abroad or in camp, but the only institution in the country that was above the issue and effects of war—the Church.

As Feudalism created a condition of greater poverty than slavery, so Emancipation exceeded Feudalism in the same process.   The freer the people became from obligation, the more they could indulge their own desires ; and these left no margin of protection from misfortune, folly, ill-health, or famine.   The more poverty grew from personal freedom of action, the less also became the obligation of the seignors to subscribe for its relief.

To return to the Church.   In the distribution of alms

the Church experienced the Natural law that there was
an equivalent to everything, and that the Poor were
grateful and willing to be reciprocative, if opportunity
occurred, for the benefits they received. It was therefore natural that the Church should turn this gratitude
to its own account. All institutions must keep their
interests in the forefront of their actions. But this is
peculiarly the case with the Church, because it believes
that its own interests are, or include, the paramount
interests of all humanity. The Church changed the
moral note into a religious one, and the gratitude and
desire to reciprocate that moved the Poor was sought to
be converted into submission to discipline and religious
observance.

From this very natural action of the Church many
curious effects flowed, all more or less obliterative of
Natural philanthropy. In the first place the establish-
ment of a permanent intermediary in philanthropy
interrupts the flow of gratitude to the proper person to
whom it is due. In Natural philanthropy the benefactor and his subject meet, and the gratitude of the one
to the other is active and direct. This gratitude is a
powerful instrument for good in the benefactor's hands,
if he wishes to use it, and it can always be depended
upon for reasonable service when wanted. But when
it becomes known that the distributor is not the real
benefactor, but only an agent performing a duty, then
there is no gratitude due to the agent, and the benefactor
to whom the gratitude is due is unknown. The Church
felt this lack of gratitude, and imperceptibly and un-
consciously, to cure it began to separate as widely from
each other as possible the Charitable and the Poor. It
was easily done in those days. The lands, the money,
and the privileges the Church received from the wealthy
on behalf of the Poor was not likely to become known
to the Poor, or if known, would soon pass from their

remembrance, and the Church would then stand in the place of the original donor, and exact its full tribute of gratitude. All simple actions that are agreeable to us soon become settled principles, and are capable of extension. The next step was to preach the doctrine of separation, *i.e.* that it was the duty of the rich to give to the Church (of course for the Poor), and their reward was the Church's blessing, and the Church dealt with the Poor as they thought proper. Here philanthropy ceased altogether. The Rich gave to the Church as a religious duty ; that the money was for the Poor or any other purpose was a matter of detail.

When the Church stood towards the Poor as their principal benefactor, it found that gratitude would not flow as freely to an impersonal institution as to an individual philanthropist. The Church is in that unfortunate position it can never see or believe itself to be in the wrong, and what it mistook for studious ingratitude was only natural effect. To stimulate the gratitude of the Poor it began a course of favouritism which finally ended in preaching the doctrine of selection. The moral code that influenced individual philanthropy could not sympathise so much with the individual whose condition was the result of his own folly, as it could with the person whose poverty was the result of unavoidable misfortune, and naturally its efforts on behalf of the one were not likely to be as full and spontaneous as the other ; but the new code declared it was the duty to help the person whose folly was attributable to himself, if he only declared his penitence, in preference to the unfortunate through no fault of his own, if he were indifferent to religion. How much of that sentiment still exists we do not know ; but forty years ago it was the accepted dogma on charity in many parts of the country. The writer's mother was a woman of strict religious training. She was very keen in her sympathy with suffering, yet a woman of cool reason and clear perception. But from her education she could be beguiled out of any and every thing giveable she possessed by a pious story of misfortune, and shut her heart sternly to cases of real suffering if associated with impiety.

The Poor were just as able and willing to make the necessary pretence of religion, when they wanted any-thing, as they are at the present day able to pass the special investigation of the distributing missions. Religion is not a necessity to their existence, and forms no part of their lives, unless when it is necessary to adopt it. If the Church could have had the patience to wait to see what gratitude the Poor were inclined to render them for their doles, taken it, much or little—it was costing them nothing—without murmur, and moulded it to the religious edification of the poor, they would have done something. But, ever impatient and dogmatic, it put its price upon the goods first, and the Poor, if they required them much, bought them with false coin, or left them alone otherwise.

The effect upon the Poor was not very great ; the effect upon religion was very degrading. Instead of being that high and holy thing unsullied by worldly thoughts or ways, it was hawked in the market. Instead of being preached to all the world, who would wish to hear, boldly but reverently and with dignity, it was offered in the streets and the slums with bribes and bonuses to induce a purchase, the very thing that made it worthless in the eyes of the Poor.

The strange metamorphoses wrought by the Church in philanthropy, whereby from being the most insigni-ficant of the parties interested, being merely an agent to fulfil the behests of the principal, it changed to a position overtopping and dominating the others, dictating the duty of the one, and discharging it to the other at its own discretion, need not be laid to its charge as an intentional design. It was the natural evolution of philanthropy on the introduction of a middleman, where Nature required none. It can be seen working every day at the present as well as in the past, because the position of middleman is so attractive to all who have tried it, or seen the inward workings of a mission, that none would think of doing without it.

" Just fancy, young man, if you are inclined to be philanthropical. You have only to get hold of a moderately attractive idea—it does not require to be too brilliant, because your friends may not be able to understand it if it is. You need not worry yourself about its practicability ; make up for the lack of that by throwing in a lot of sentiment—the more useless and impracticable the sentiment the better. Always remember that the people who are going to support your mission only know the sentimental side of the philanthropical question. It is the Poor who know the practical side ; but they can be ignored.

Your idea once formed, you have only to talk it over with your friends. Should any of these be of a practical nature, and show you that you are overlooking obvious facts, prove to him that it is the ennobling principle of your scheme, the elevating strength of its natural virtue, the attractive force of its spirituality, that you look to, to irresistibly overcome all difficulties. He will say no more, and your other friends, who may have mentally agreed with him will be glad they did not say anything, and will answer, " I believe you are right." Having formed a little band of sympathetic, but uninfluential supporters, your next move is to write the subject up in the correspondence columns of the press ; your friends of course taking their share.

You will not have long to wait until some prominent philanthropist will send you a note inviting you to meet him to talk over the matter. This is the tide that leads on to fortune. If you are wise you will not talk so much about your scheme as about yourself. It will be upon the impression you create personally that the success of your scheme will depend. In all probability it may be the fiftieth or sixtieth plan the good gentleman has helped to begin ; in all probability he would not understand your scheme if you attempted to explain it to him. He will be mainly interested in who and what you are. It will be your own fault therefore if you deceive him. You must be religious, enthusiastic, sentimental, and, above all, you must be a firm believer in the interference of the Divine Spirit in worldly things, for that is to be the guiding force of your plan, and the shield for all your folly, ignorance, and mischief. It does not matter whether you believe in Divine interposition or not : they do. Why we say they, we will explain.

In all the large towns we have resided in, the great cities of London, New York, &c., excepted, we have found that the wealthy philanthropists who make a profession of philanthropy are a small coterie that herd together because of this bond they have in common. They seem to be a people who have got the idea that a certain portion of their income must be spent yearly on philanthropical purposes, whether these purposes exist or have to be made for the occasion. Being wealthy, they do no philanthropical work themselves, but subscribe and patronise. They know nothing about the Poor, and would like to know even less, if that were possible. There is no pain or distress of the Poor that they see or suffer from, and therefore seek to remove. Their philanthropy is purely of a spiritual form. They are intensely religious, and hate impiety, intemperance, immorality, &c., and they, with all the rest of us, are taught that these evils flourish more profusely among the lower than the other classes. They cannot even trace where they personally or socially suffer from the

habits of the Poor; their quarrel is with vice, and they
are willing to lend a not over-critical ear to any scheme
that is meant to contend with it. They are great
believers in God's grace as a regenerating agent, partly
because of their religious training, partly because not
one in fifty of the schemes they are asked to support
has any other excuse for its existence.

As the distributing mission advertises to the Poor
where they can get food and clothes for nothing, so
these wealthy philanthropists by their actions advertise
to the charlatan and bogus evangelist where they may
get ready and remunerative victims. In private circles
they are called the milch-cows of philanthropy. Nothing
is too preposterous for their gullibility to swallow; no
amount of failure brings experience. They stand in
their stalls and their udders are ready to be sucked, be
it by the quack doctor who professes to cure intemperance with a pill, or the Yankee preacher who is
going to destroy vice by preaching during the week-
days to the most religious classes in the city.

The decision as to taking up your philanthropical
scheme, we have said, will rest upon the effect you personally make. If you play your cards properly, then
you will be reported as "sincere." "Such a good
young man, so earnest, so enthusiastic, so full of the
true spirit of philanthropy." Then they will agree that
they must do something for you; they must take up
your scheme and see what comes of it. Now comes
the real pleasure of existence. You are asked to after-
noons, to teas, to dinners, and to evenings among
these wealthy people to talk the matter over. If you
are unmarried and good looking, all the young ladies
will be *so* sympathetic; while the elder folk will be
courteous and attentive.

The next stage is the first public meeting, not a large
one, but so enthusiastic! All devoted philanthropists

come to applaud and approve. You may be a little nervous when you find yourself upon a platform for the first time, next to the chairman, who may be the mayor, or the bishop, or a nobleman from the neighbouring county. Your nervousness will soon pass away when you find every word or two vociferously applauded, and before you sit down you will have come to believe you are a born orator. You will have drunk of the poison of public applause, and you will be longing and itching for further opportunities. You will dream of public meetings, and every trivial matter to be settled you will require a public meeting to settle it.

After your first preliminary meeting there are congratulations and introductions all round. The committee has to be formed, and during the process the invitations to the houses of the wealthy roll in. You are enjoying yourself immensely, but they see it in a different light; they call it hard work, and say they never saw any young man work so hard and spend himself so unselfishly.

You may be beginning to wonder where it will all end, but you need have no fear. Your committee will do everything for you, they will find everything, the money will be coming in. You will not even be asked to take a working part in your own scheme; all that will be done by paid servants. You will be required for far more important (and pleasant) duties. You will be consulted about the purchase or hire of the hall, the engagement of the staff, the districts to be experimented upon. You will enjoy the luxury of casting other people's money about in large and generous sums. Finally, when the opening meeting takes place, when all who are of any importance have attended to wish your scheme " God speed," when it has been prayed for and blessed, and afterwards when the oratory and enthusiasm have been turned on full blast, when every person is congratulatory and hopeful, you yourself will, for the first time, begin to doubt—if you have not doubted before.

Such as the Church made the mission it remains without change to this day. It is not because the system worked so admirably that there was found no room for improvement. It is not from any lack of inventive genius among the generations of philanthropists that have come and gone since the system became an institution among us. It is not that new forms of distress and new social difficulties have not appeared in the lives of the Poor. It is from the simple reason that when one is satisfied with existing methods, his mind does not occupy itself with thoughts of change. The position of middleman is so agreeable that there is not likely to be any change so long as missions and their peculiar form of philanthropy last.

The destruction of individual philanthropy made philanthropy a virtue of the Rich. All who had not a surplus of means were excluded from its exercise. The mission will tell you that such is not the fact ; that the smallest donation will be thankfully received, &c. These are mere conscience quibbles. The record of every-day experience is different. The public advertisement of subscriptions alone, prevent all but those who can contribute a respectable sum from entering the lists. The institution that is informing us daily of its requirements, amounting to hundreds and thousands, does not persuade the person of a few shillings that he can be of any important service. But the money question is not the question ; it is bad in philanthropy, root and branch. *Those who cannot subscribe believe themselves to be free from philanthropical obligation.* We leave it then to the arithmetician to make out this problem. Say there are seven millions of people in the district called London ; say one-sixth of these are able-bodied people

of both sexes. Say that in London there are not more
than seven thousand people who yearly subscribe to a
voluntary mission. Say whether all the money subscribed by these seven—or we will be generous and say
seventy—thousand could effect more good than the
individual service of a million of people among the
Poor? If there were no mission, every one would have
grown up to his personal responsibility to human
suffering. The fact, of course, must be looked at that
the classes do not mix. But on the other hand, if such
an artificial form of philanthropy can be taught, as that
we give money to remedy distress we know nothing
about and do not suffer from, might we not be as easily
taught the duty of visiting and mixing with our poorer
brethren? What the good to them would be, arising
from such personal sympathy, may be easily guessed—
there would be no poverty or distress in a month, but
what was absolutely unavoidable. What the effect
upon ourselves would be is inconceivable. If we reduced ourselves to one class, there would only be one
standard of religion and morality, and it would be that
of the better class. To those who have spent their money
as water in trying to make the Poor religious and moral
we offer that suggestion for them to ponder over.

When the Church preached philanthropy as a religious duty, it raised the duty to the Church's
schemes, the mission to the poor among them,
to a higher consideration than the objects for which
they were instituted. And this remains to this day. To
the missionary, the welfare of the mission is the first
concern ; the object for which it was established the
next. To every Church the welfare of its institutions
is greater than the purposes they are meant to serve.
We heard of an amusing instance of this the other day.
A gentleman met a friend whose business place is in one
of the lowest quarters of the town. The friend told him

that from this cause he knew nearly every inhabitant in
his street. They were not a very reputable lot, but the
principal business of most of them was to play upon the
public sympathy. Among them were street-singers,
beggars, musicians, the lame, the halt, and the blind in
outward appearance. The friend kept the gentleman
laughing at their many devices to deceive the public—
"fakes" whose triumphs the Poor themselves enjoyed
immensely. But among this unworthy crowd, he told
the gentleman, there were some real cases of distress,
some people who refused these unworthy means of
making money, and who preferred to toil on and keep
their sorrows to themselves. The gentleman gave the
friend a five-pound note, and told him to use it among
the Poor as he thought fit. The knowledge of this
transaction came to the ears of some members of the
church to which the gentleman belonged. The action
gave considerable offence. The parson and some of
the principal men in connection with the church took
him to task for not giving the money through their
own mission. The gentleman's defence was that the
money was for the Poor, and every penny of it would
be used to its full value. That was no defence. His
duty, he was told, was to the mission of the church.
It also had Poor, and required money ; and how could
it do its work unless it was supported? The gentleman
pleaded again that to give his money to the Poor must
surely be the same as giving it to a mission to give to
the Poor. But the church managers knew it was a very
different thing, and were by no means appeased.
They could not tell him the true reason, namely, that
the maintenance of the mission was more important to
them than the relief of the Poor ; that had he given
his money to the mission its own necessities would
first be provided for, and the balance go in charity,
and in charity to those only who would acknowledge

E

the mission, not the gentleman, as their benefactor, and be grateful accordingly ; or, as an old lady put it, "Giving away all that money to people they did not know anything about." Here, such artificial philanthropy as there was was subservient to the glory of the mission.

This exaltation of the mission, especially in those towns where there was some sectarian rivalry, culminated in the production and manufacture of a new class of philanthropists. These we call the Bumblepuppy philanthropists, because we can find no other name for them. We saw one day a book called "Bumblepuppy," and on opening its pages for an explanation, we were informed that Bumblepuppy was in all respects a game like whist, so like, that the players believed themselves to be playing whist while they were only playing Bumblepuppy, as they played in ignorance, or defiance, of the known principles of whist, or both. From trivial things to serious, these philanthropists act towards philanthropy in exactly like manner. They call themselves philanthropists, and believe themselves to be so. They act outwardly as other philanthropists act, but they are ignorant, or defiant, of its known principles, and they are proud of their ignorance or defiance. They are the emissaries of a special mission or "cause" which holds the first and only place in their hearts. They make no pretence to love the Poor ; they are at war with all who differ from them, and whatever punishment their imprudence brings upon them they glory in as a form of martyrdom. No reason can affect them, no argument convince, no prayer restrain.

These people do not go among the Poor, because there is no evil to cure in their own and other classes, but because they believe their social position should have weight with the Poor, while it gives them no influence over their own people. One of these

philanthropists may have "religion" for his cause, or
"temperance." His next door neighbour may be his
antithesis—infidel, bibulous. The philanthropist knows
that these circumstances give him no right to enter his
friend's house at any time he may wish, to lecture
and admonish him upon his habits. They are not
likely to be friends, from their different habits, but
they will continue quite neighbourly notwithstanding.
Their wives may be in the same set, their children
play together, or be at the same school. They exchange
the compliments of the day when they meet in the
morning. They walk to the car together and talk about
the weather and business. And should they meet in
the afternoon they may walk home together.

Now see the Bumblepuppyist among the Poor.
Every spark of civility, common courtesy, and consideration is left behind. He enters the houses of the
Poor without any other preliminary than a peremptory
knock, not even that if the door be open. He has no
hesitation in interrupting their conversation, breaking
up their privacy, giving his advice upon their actions.
He opens his subject irrespective of their time and inclination, and if he knows of any recent occasion of
backsliding among them, he admonishes them as if he
were their priest and confessor. Should they show
any resentment, he has no hesitation in condemning
them, and drawing the attention of others to what he
calls their hardened and depraved state, and in the
Meeting Hall in the evening he advertises their name
and story as a warning to others.

Who is this person who takes upon himself to go
among the Poor and call over their sins to them?
Is he their judge, their lord, or master? If
you ask him by what authority he acts, he will
blasphemously say, "In the name of God"; and to
avoid further blasphemy you are silent.

The Poor hate this person with a bitterness that is not easily describable ; but what is more unfortunate is, that he is the cause of them to a large extent hating everything and everybody that is associated with mission work.   In forming our opinion of types we are not wholly acquainted with, it is the exaggerations that impress themselves strongest upon our memory.   The Bumblepuppy is the extreme of anything that professes to associate itself with philanthropy, and because of the annoyance and irritation he produces in the Poor, when the word " missionary" is mentioned it is his form that is imaged in their minds.   They know he dare not act towards his equals as he acts towards them.   They know he is taking advantage of his social position, or he dare not act as he does.   The Poor are as amenable to reason as any other class if approached in the proper manner.   They are as accessible as any other class, and by the same avenues.   They are as ready to listen to anyone who has anything to say to them, and requests to be heard in the customary way ; but they see all these preliminary social forms daily thrust aside in their case, and by people in whom they recognise no authority, and to whom they owe no allegiance.   Flesh and blood will not stand that any person unauthorised and unsolicited should come amongst us to denounce our habits, interfere with our pleasures, condemn our lives, and do all in his power to destroy our happiness, and expect that we should take his doings calmly beside.

Of all the excrescences that the evolution of philanthropy has produced since the advent of the middleman, this person is truly the most injurious.

CHAPTER IV

The Political Philanthropist and the Claim of Right—The Poor are
not political—When politics were thrust upon them they had
nothing but personal wants—The aspiring politician offered
these philanthropically—Workmen claimed them as rights—
Political rivalry admitted the right—Labourist demands.

THE Poor, not being given to intellectual pursuits, are
not political. Politics are a mental study ; they lie purely
in the intellectual region, some people calling them
the study of the science of good government. It has
been the misfortune of the poor that they have had
politics thrust upon them, and of the rest of the country
that they do not know how to use the privilege.

When the first Reform Bill was passed, it was after
years of agitation by an intelligent, educated people,
who demanded to have a share in the guiding of the
country for which they were so heavily taxed. It was
looked upon in those days as a very liberal bill. But
the basis of its franchise was a money one, while the
true qualification for politics is political knowledge or
education. Every person who joined the agitation for
reform believed himself a properly qualified person to
judge of the great questions of the day. The Reform

Bill, so to speak, run its shears through the mass and separated those who had so much money from those who had a penny less, and left the question of brains alone.   Those left outside the pale were no better off than before, their grievances were not redressed, and all the evils from the standpoint of the principles they were contending for remained the same.   An agitation for reform may be said to have sprung up from the day the Reform Bill passed into law.   The numbers were at first few : the scissors had taken away a great many, and it was twenty to thirty years before the numbers became great enough to be again a political " Voice " that must be heeded.

The second Reform Bill sank down into the social body as far as the intellectual line, and from thenceforward there was nobody left outside the political circle who had any desire to get in because of their political knowledge.   So far there was nobody left outside to agitate for a further extension of the franchise, nor would there have been such an agitation from them till Doomsday.   The agitation came from the inside.   Not from those who were in want of it, but from those who wished them to have it.   The pleasure of swaying large masses by shibboleths, of holding them by playing to their prejudices, and by exchanging principle for popularity, was a temptation ever before the hard-driven politician.   The hour of stress came, either to the politician or the party, and the floodgates were opened, and the government of the country passed into the keeping of the least intelligent portion of the community, under the advice and guidance of the next least cultivated portions, the portions that produce the agitator and the wealthy parliamentary aspirant.   The one advises the Poor what they should do, and the other offers to do what they advise.

It is one thing to entrust your vessel to a person who

has studied navigation and practised seamanship, and
another to put the tiller in the hands of one who knows
nothing about a helm, and does not want to know.
The first can keep the course that is given him until
another is set, the other becomes pleased with the
power he has over the vessel, and delighted at being
able to make it go where he chooses. Such a change has
been noticeable in our legislation since Demos was king.

In the previous extensions of the voting privilege the
newly franchised looked upon themselves as men taken
into partnership with those already franchised, for the
purpose of assisting to govern the nation. They knew
the broad principles of government that were observed
by both contending parties. They were familiar with
the political questions of the day, and they were prepared to lend a deliberative voice on the subjects under
parliamentary consideration. They simply swelled the
bulk of parties without altering their politics. It was
impossible to expect our latest legislators to do so ;
they had no preparation. Yet those most interested in
including them within the parliamentary circle fully
hoped they would act as their predecessors acted.
What they did do was, they refused to amalgamate.
They knew nothing about parliamentary precedent ;
they cared less about parliamentary principles. They
were ignorant of economics, and therefore suspected
them. Under the fostering care of their agitators they
became a class by themselves, and a party by themselves, with the sole purpose of benefiting their own
condition at no matter whose cost, or of any consideration for the country.

These newly franchised had no previous experience in
acting together unless during strikes, and it was not to
be wondered at that their parliamentary action was the
same as their industrial action when on strike. A
strike has no principle, and admits of no argument.

It is a simple declaration of will, either on the part of
the employers or the employed. But having once been
made it rises to the height of a dogma or faith, from
which all reason is excluded, and for which all things
must be endured.

The parliamentary legislation of the working classes
is only their industrial demands writ large. Instead
of having to deal with an individual employer they had
in parliament all the employers, and any person, be he
Whig or Tory, who sought to remonstrate, reason, or
advise with them on any of their demands was at once
put down as a friend or sympathiser with the capitalist,
and an enemy of theirs. Politics, so far as they were
the science of good government, ceased to exist
because the new legislators knew nothing about them,
but, like the unskilled navigator, they were pleased to
find they had control of a machine that could do many
things for them that it would be too troublesome to
do for themselves. A class that was capable, for years
before they had any legislative power, of settling satisfactorily the one primary condition of all labour—
wages—sought to occupy the parliament of the
nation in fixing such minor details for them as the
hours they should work, the compensation for accidents,
the position and safety of the machinery, the healthiness of the factory and the occupation, and such-like
trifling matters. Shades of Chatham, Pitt, and Fox!
To think that the great British Parliament, the mother
of all parliaments, was now reduced to being the valet
and charwoman of the great unwashed ; that the
principal occupation of between 600 and 700 gentlemen
of wealth and education was to arrange the details of
Mr. Demos's employment when he chooses to work.
To fix when he shall begin in the morning ; to see he
does not work five minutes past his time at dinner or
evening. To go before him, and see that the place has

been properly swept out and cleaned, that the machinery
has all been covered up, the tools and tackle tested,
and all dangerous weapons hid away. Then remain
behind and clear up after him, as he might want to
work to-morrow again. By and by parliament will be
employed passing legislation to supply the workman
with his meals, to help him on with his coat when his
work is done, and drive him home when he feels tired.
But while he puts parliament to the task of settling for
him the minor details of his labour, he retains in his
own hands the two important—all-important principles
of labour—the settlement of the wages, and the right
to strike when he pleases. These things he will trust
to no silly parliament to interfere with.

There are many wealthy but weak gentlemen to
whom the social distinction of being a member of
parliament was something worth doing a good deal for.
In the days of a more restricted electorate these gentlemen dare not have presumed to aspire to such an
honour. Then, the constituencies demanded social
position, local influence, and a reasonable amount of
political knowledge. Now that the constituencies, or
their caucuses, supply the politics themselves there is
more room for selection. And the politics that *are*
supplied can only be subscribed to by a person to whom
a seat in parliament is of more importance than any
political principle. It was a sore position for these
gentlemen to find themselves in. They had to support
in public, principles and measures that their whole life's
experience, convictions, and prejudices held to be rank
heresies. They could not defend them with any heart
against their political opponents ; they could not justify
them to their own friends. At last, when the position
was becoming intolerable, they found relief by abandon-
ing all defence, and assuming the high ground of
philanthropy. The Poor, they said, were not to be

treated by the ordinary hard-and-fast laws of civilisation. The laws of God and Nature, under which all men are born to work, were in their case to be abrogated. But as there were difficulties in the way of doing so, they would be content in the meantime, if they were interpreted in a wide and generous spirit as regards the Poor, but the Poor only. They were hereafter to be elevated to the position of a sacred class. They were to receive always more than they gave; they were to be allowed to reap where they had not sown; and if any man owed one of them fifty he was to pay him a hundred.

The making labour profitable to the employer so that he might be able to give employment was not now the one thing necessary; that was a too coarse and vulgar way of looking at the relations between capital and labour. Labour was to be made happy and contented first, and the employer was an ungrateful fellow who looked for any other reward than the happiness of his *employés*. The wage basis was not to be fixed as heretofore, as the workman's proportion of profit, taking he and the proprietor as partners in the manufacture of an article, but on the workman's requirements for amusements and leisure. The hours of labour were to be arranged so that no man's day's work should fatigue him that he could not properly and freshly enjoy his pleasures in the evening; to do so were slavery. The parliamentary philanthropist never tired himself with *his* day's labour; why should the workman? It was discovered by the same gentlemen that the wage-earners had been shamefully treated in the past, and to make amends we could not do too much for them now.

When philanthropy is supposed to be the guide of one's actions, discussion of them by the ordinary laws of experience are excluded. The opponents of the parliamentary philanthropist dared not now laugh at his

crude and selfish schemes ; to do so was to laugh at his
goodness of heart, his sympathy with the Poor, his
philanthropy ; and to laugh at a person's philanthropy
is in the eyes of some as bad as to laugh at his religion
—especially the people who expect to benefit by his
good intentions. On the contrary, they found themselves in a very awkward fix. They could not do
without their share of the new vote, and they were now
deprived of appealing to the masses upon the grounds
of principle, sentiment, experience, or progress. None
of these could hold the field against philanthropy, and
so to philanthropy they also had to come, and out-
herod Herod in their coming.

The political tie is the next strongest one to the
social ; much stronger than the religious or educational
ties. For one person affected by a new religious idea
hundreds are moved by a new political one. With both
the great political parties of the State preaching
philanthropy on the platform, in the press, and in every
drawing-room in the country, the nation has become
saturated (to use a favourite expression of the politicians) with the idea of political philanthropy.

The difference between political and private philanthropy is that the former has no power of personal
discrimination of cases, no power of stopping when the
occasion for their services are past except in special
cases, and that each philanthropical suggestion becomes
a " Claim of Right," and must be presented and argued
as such before it can pass into legislation.

The Poor, like all other people, hate the name of
Charity. It is suggestive of dependence and gratitude.
One cannot win their suffrages by offering them any
amelioration of their condition as the gratuitous gift of
himself or his party ; it must be offered to them as a
long-withheld act of justice, as a right, and an equitable
adjustment of the benefits of government.

The Claim of Right at present of the wage-earner is a pretty lengthy one, and there is not an item in it all that the workman found out for himself; not an item that pressed upon his daily life to the extent of being a nuisance he would wish to have removed. All of them were found out for him by the agitator, or suggested to him by the political philanthropist. In addition to his hours of labour and all its petty details that we have just mentioned, there is the grand principle that it is the duty of the country, in other words, that it is the duty of every person and class in the country, to see that the conditions of life of the wage-earner are never changed for the worse. The paramount duty of the nation is to place the workman above the vicissitudes of fortune. What no person can do for himself, the country is to combine to do for this favoured class. He was to be insured of suitable, comfortable, warm, roomy, cleanly, sanitary houses. He was entitled to a reasonable amount of leisure for amusement and entertainment; he had a right to a generous diet of good unadulterated food, and warm clothing, and a holiday to coast or country for himself and family during the summer. He was to have a wage that would freely provide him with all this, and a margin for exceptional occasions. He was to have this wage for working less hours than at present. He was to be kept free from competition, especially alien labour, so that his wage would not be interfered with; he was to have a guarantee that it should never be reduced, and the Government or municipalities were to keep open workshops for his relief, so that he should never be out of employment. He was to be freed from all care and responsibility about himself. He was to be rewarded if he got hurt, maintained if he fell sick, and relieved if he chose to remain idle; and if he lived to be sixty years old he need not work any more.

That the Poor should ask these things, they are to be excused. They know nothing of politics, and they are being incited and urged to do so by members of both political parties as their right. That they stopped short of demanding that they should not work at all shows they have still some moderation left, because that is the only true and natural desire they have themselves. But that there are educated men who for the sake of parliamentary prestige can be found to encourage them in rushing to their ruin, shows to what a low ebb politics have come.

The number of protections that the working classes are seeking to hedge round their present conditions of labour with denote a fear that they have reached the economical line of true value. Every person of course will have his own opinion on the subject, but we take our conclusions from the workman's own fears. His anxiety to be protected from a reduction, by making an irreducible standard ; his fears of competition by aliens ; his dread that his work may become unprofitable to private employers in his anxiety to see Government and municipal workshops opened ; all these denote that he feels his present conditions of life are higher than he could maintain them by his own labour in open competition. The workman feels this, and despite the assurances of the agitator, and the benevolent patronage of the political philanthropist, he knows his own feelings are a better guide to the true state of affairs.

The workman knows better than any other person, because he sees what his advisers do not see. He sees all around him, not only alien labour, but native labour ready and willing to work for his employer for less money than he is doing ; not only labour outside his Unions, but within—half the work of their " Unions " and " Societies " is the coercion of their own members.

The raising of workmen's wages to an abnormal

height, either naturally or artificially, is to attract to
that high wage all the workmen who have been earning
less.   If the increase affects all workmen alike in the
country, as at one time in the United States and our
Australian colonies, then it draws the workmen from all
other countries where wages are lower : if it affects
one trade only, it draws men from other trades who
believe themselves capable of the work (and there are
a great many tradesmen acquainted with more than one
occupation) ; if it affects a trade in a town, then that
town is the Mecca of all the workmen in the country
who work at that trade.   There is nothing human can
stop that law of attraction.   Autocratic, Democratic,
and Republican governments have all tried in vain.   It
is part of the greatest law of life, " The best conditions
for its own existence" ; it works in all life automatically—
even the owner of the life could not stop it—and it is
exhibited in the wage-earner by finding the best market
for his labour, no matter where it may be.

The attempt to raise artificially the wages of any
trade, is to first draw more men to that trade than
there is work for, and then the competition that sets in
brings back the wages sometimes to a lower standard
than before the rise.   It is always the stranger who
takes the lower wage first, and the resident for whose
benefit the attempt was made is left in idleness.

The old philanthropists have been for about fifty
years teaching the working classes that all virtue, or
rather all the virtues these working classes in the
opinion of the philanthropists lacked, must first be
cultivated by thrift, self-denial, prudence, and general
restraint.   Only through the exercise of these personal
qualities could virtue spring ; but through these all
goodness, religion, virtue, morality, etc., would naturally
flow, and the fear of poverty and distress would pass
away for ever.   To use their wages with prudence, to

see that every farthing spent was not only spent upon a
proper object, but made to go as far as possible.   To
practice self-restraint and self-control against mere
personal indulgence.   Rather to do without, for sake of
saving a little each week, than spend all.   These and
similar recommendations were the staple advice of the
old virtuous school of philanthropy.   If the regeneration of man, and the cure for, or protection against
poverty, lie in the exercise of these qualities, how are
they to be fostered under the new philanthropical
teaching?   Already one of the most popular of workmen's agitators has laughed and sneered at thrift, and
has contemptuously expressed himself about Smiles, a
writer on the subject.   The workman is to be an
irresponsible being, and the government is to supply
him, without any effort on his part, with all that the
exercise of these virtues of prudence, thrift, and self-
denial are supposed to bring to their disciples.   We
wonder if the two schools of philanthropy are aware of
the antagonism of their teachings!   We wonder if the
parliamentary philanthropist would prefer to see a
nation the product of his own philosophy, or one of the
older teachers'!

The gentlemen who have been so assiduous in
teaching the labourer what his "rights" are, have not
been very explicit in informing him how they are to be
reached.   On this subject they are studiously vague
or discreetly silent.   Yet this to the workman is the
most important part.   At present the wages of unskilled labour could not attain all the good things
entered in his schedule; it is doubtful if even the
average wage of skilled labour is sufficient to purchase
them.   What a state of perpetual discontent and
unrest must the life of the workman be in, who is told
he is entitled to a certain life of comfort, and yet his
wages are unable to procure it for him!   The anger of

that discontent must be turned against some one. Not the agitator, nor the parliamentary philanthropist. Oh! no,—the employer! The unpolitical workman can see no further than the man who pays him his wages, and does not pay him enough. Enough for what? Not the work he has done, but the ideal life he is told should be his. Within the past ten years what strikes have occurred from this reason, and this alone! What thousands of pounds have the workmen thrown away in wages! What thousands of pounds of profit have they deprived the employers of, and through them the country! What trades they have ruined, diverted, and made wholly unprofitable because of this belief in an ideal life without the possibility of an ideal wage! And this is supposed to be a cure for poverty.

The unpolitical workman is not expected to know his true relation to his employer; but his advisers, the agitator and the politician, should; or should not interfere with the life and economy of the artizan at all. They should know that the higher wages are forced above their natural level the more constricted the labour market becomes. For every shilling the men of a trade succeed in forcing up their wages, they also force so many tradesmen into idleness. By reducing the profit of the employer on his hire of labour they are reducing his power of hire. If he be a manufacturer, he is less capable of meeting a falling market, and has no recourse but to shut his works, while others can keep theirs still going. He cannot, like the others, manufacture stock in dull times; his cost price will be so high, the market is sure to be against him. He has to wait; and can do nothing unless at the short periods, when the market rises to high tide. When the employer is not a manufacturer, but an employer of labour, say as a contractor, engineer, mechanic, etc., he is forced out of competitive work, and must depend wholly on local repairs, additions, etc. Where he might be able to employ hundreds and thousands, he is reduced to tens.

London at the present day, where the doctrine of workman's rights has been most assiduously and acceptably preached, is known in the case of many trades to be suffering from artificial wages, and it is only the enormous size of the place that deprives people, especially the working man, from seeing clearly the great contraction of its trade in these departments.

From the number of its factories and workshops of all kinds, London is a huge repairing shop, capable of permanently supporting an army of workmen— builders, engineers, mechanics, etc., to attend to its local wants. These local wants are at the mercy of local tradesmen, who are again the victims of the workmen and their societies. No matter what the cost of these repairs, additions, alterations, or the rate of men's wages, they have to be done and paid for. But it is also known, because of the rate of workmen's wages, and other irksome conditions enforced by their Unions, London is entirely thrown out of the market for new work; not only new work for the country, or for foreign countries, but new work for its own use. Its highly paid ideal-lived artizans have to stand aside and see provincial workmen build its bridges, its ferries, its factories and their machinery. Anything and everything that can be put beyond the local tradesmen is being got from the provinces. The shipping of the world goes up the Thames, and should, under favourable circumstances, require for overhaul and repairs almost as many engineers and artificers as are already in London; but we have been informed by more than one shipowner, that the general instructions to captains bound for London, is, that if they have another port of discharge in the kingdom, they are not to spend a

penny on the ship in London. We do not know anything about its railways, but, like its ships, we suppose
there are more locomotives, carriages, and trucks enter
and leave London every day than any other place—
at least in Europe. But we have never heard of it
having any prominent locomotive works or repairing
sheds. Probably in this case also, everything that can
run on wheels, or be carried, is removed beyond the
influence of the London workman. Truly the Claim of
Right is like a leprosy from which all business flees.

CHAPTER V

The old and the new philanthropists : comparison—The indifference of the Poor to philanthropical teaching—The philanthropist's attempt to rouse the Poor by preaching the Gospel of
Discontent—The Poor accepted the new doctrine as the
foundation of Socialism.

THE ways of the new philanthropist throw a strange
reflection on the ways, the beliefs, and the methods of
the old. The old philanthropist never thought of
interfering with the economy of the lives of the Poor
in whom he was interested, unless to the extent of
advising them of a better method (in his opinion) of
how to spend their wages. As the Poor had no political
power then, there were none found to gratuitously
mislead them as to what government should do for
them. In those days, say forty years ago, government
was not expected to do anything for anybody but tax
them, and in that no one found any source of relief.
The old philanthropist taught the workman that even
the wages he worked for and received should be looked
upon as the bounty of Providence, for which he should
be grateful, and which he should dispose of with the
ever-present feeling of having been specially favoured.

F 2

It was the lack of this guiding feeling in the spending of their wages, to which the old philanthropist and his kind attributed all the misery and poverty of the lower classes.

It was not that the poorer classes did not earn enough money to keep them, but that they spent it wrongfully.

Holding these views—and, to a certain extent, they were the true ones—they saw no other guiding and controlling influence to keep the Poor in the proper path but religion. It was contemptuously held against this class of philanthropists, that if you asked them for bread they gave you a tract. It was a pity that their philosophy was so liable to abuse. People who exhibited no striking or ostentatious morality in their own lives, became suddenly censorious and rigidly critical in their neighbour's ways and mode of living immediately that neighbour showed signs of distress, and the necessity for relief. These people brought religious philanthropy into disrepute by their actions. But these people have existed from all time, and have always been bringing something into disrepute—generally the finest or most sacred of human emotions—to cloak their own selfishness. But in ninety-nine cases out of a hundred, a tract was more serviceable to the necessitous than a loaf. In the first place it was for want of a tract or disregard of its teachings that they came to their unenviable plight. What is the use of repairing a man's dogcart for him if he still determines to drive down hill with it again to the inevitable smash, and refuses all advice to take the level and the safe way? Better let the cart lie than waste your time and material only to have your work to do over again. Of two men receiving the same wages, and the conditions of whose domestic arrangements are much the same, does it not make life a little harder for the one who works by the "tract," subordinating all his personal

desires for the sake of spending wisely and thriftily, and
saving carefully, as if his weekly wages were so many
talents he had to give an account of " to the uttermost
farthing," to find his neighbour light his pipe with his
" tract," and with his earnings satisfy every desire as
it arises until his money is spent, then go and borrow
from his wiser neighbour? Temporary relief involves
no principle, teaches no lesson, solves no difficulty, and
to those who only seek to relieve their own distress at
the sight of another's, it is well ; but to those pious
philanthropists, the effect they hoped to produce by
their religious teaching was an absolute cure for
poverty, and to them temporary relief was as insignificant as to the physician who meant to eradicate
the disease.

  If the principle is to be established, that distress must
be relieved because it is Distress, then its relief must
become paramount to personal possession. This is the
root-germ of socialism, the gospel of irresponsibility,
and encouragement to spendthriftness. It is also the
doctrine preached by the new philanthropist, only he
thinks he saves himself from the charge of socialism
by throwing the burden of relief, not upon those who
have the means (himself among others), but upon the
government or the municipality.

  The older philanthropists knew that no man could
see or suffer distress without seeking to relieve it, and
that was sufficient for temporary purposes ; but their
purpose was to protect against its recurrence and to
destroy it. They believed in and so taught their
poorer brethren the beauties of holiness, the security
and protection of self-denial, the comfort of cleanliness,
the strength and confidence derived from education, the
heart's-ease of a moral and law-abiding life. Who
would dare to talk to the poorer classes now of their
religion, but their own friends of the Salvation Army?

Do not they spend their Sundays and evenings teaching their betters Scepticism, Agnoticism, Freethought, Bob Ingersoll, Tom Paine, The Rights of Man, etc., etc.? Who dare insult the workman by hinting at self-denial? The retort comes quick—" Give us enough to practise self-denial with." But in the past, before the latest franchise, this stream of goodly talk by godly men went on night after night in mission quarters.

To see clearly in one's own mind a cure for such a distressful sore on the social body as poverty, to preach it day and night to unheeding ears, and to find the most indifferent of all to our prelections were the greatest sufferers from the evil, was enough to try the temper and patience of even a philanthropist. The wall of indifference that lies naturally between the giver and receiver of advice towered up here also, high as the Alps, impenetrable as granite. The plan could be demonstrated to be successful as easily as two and two make four. The people for whose advantage it was specially devised were bribed to come and hear it explained. Their sympathies were enlisted by presents and refreshments. They came, they took the presents, they listened and agreed the system was both efficacious and desirable, and then went on their own old way. The plan had everything to recommend it but one—it was not Natural.

Nature through the Poor, as through every other living form, is continually crying for rest, and not for labour, and all the good things offered to the Poor by the pious philanthropists, both male and female, had that misfortune ; they entailed upon the Poor extra labour while they only sought rest.

Even to the person of religious instincts the attendance at public services entails extra labour, but to a class without religious instincts or religious education none but themselves can tell what an effort it requires.

The brain that has been compressed all day during work is liberated and relieved from concentration the minute work is done. Every step homeward the workman feels to be a step lighter and easier, because the brain is beginning to unwarp itself, and act in sympathy with the body's physical motion instead of as before, controlling it. To attempt to manacle the brain again into a religious mood is more than is possible to thousands of educated gentlemen, let alone the weary worker. That is a mental hindrance we have all felt. The rest was equally insuperable, physically. The lives of the Poor, both male and female, are fully occupied, and they have no room for extra labour ; and further, their hours were filled up under a law called "The economy of Effort," and to follow the advice of the philanthropist would require an expenditure of exertion from which Nature recoils. In other words, the life offered by the philanthropist may have been, and doubtless was, best, but it was not easiest. We are all striving, not for the best, but the easiest life, only we are not always conscious of the fact. It is only now and then we awake and take ourselves to task, and determine to strive for the better instead of the easier. The better life looks beautiful, and we think it easy ; yet what tremendous energy and will-power we require to accomplish so little of it ! And little as it is, it is more than we can permanently retain. How can it be otherwise? Nature demands of us the easiest form of existence, and without our knowing it she has been utilising all our forces, all *her forces* in us, to that end. She has directed our tastes and our habits, our likes and our dislikes, our judgments and opinions, all into this one channel of personal easement, and it is not one small thing but our whole existence that is to be combated by the change. Thus day after day we delight in habits that we know are not good for us. We persist in habits our friends

assure us are hurtful, and all our defence of them is
that they do *us* no harm, and our consciences are not
altogether satisfied with the truth of our answer. We
call in physicians when we have made ourselves too
sick to pursue our usual habits, and after the first
wave of fear and apprehension is past, we cannot
even take the trouble to follow their directions. And
yet we wonder that the Poor do not turn their lives
topsy-turvy at our request, abandon habits formed by
Nature for laborious ones of the philanthropist's, and
turn their evening's rest into another day of toil for
their own improvement !

A philanthropist was caught in a shower coming
home from a mission meeting. His wife, who was very
solicitous of his health, was anxious he should change
his clothes as a precaution against cold. He had
excited himself somewhat at the meeting ; he had
hurried home. The fire in the sitting-room was bright
and cheerful ; his easy chair lay near very invitingly.
All that could be brought him in the shape of dry
clothes and that could be changed in the room he
changed ; but when it came to his trousers it was a
different matter. He would have to leave his cosy
warm chair and go upstairs to a cold bedroom and
make the exchange there. He found, therefore, "his
trousers were not so wet as he had first supposed ; they
were not wet through and through ; his underclothing
was quite dry ; he would not need to change." Of
course he was the only person of that opinion. Next
morning he had a sore throat, and then inflammation
of the lungs. Ten days afterwards, when his friends
were allowed to see him, he told us what excited him
at the meeting. "The working man," he said, "do
all you can for him, toil for him as you will,
will not lift his little finger to help himself ; will not
move hand or foot for his own good. It is simply

maddening ! " And he did not see the similarity of his own action !

The philanthropist, of course, did not know he was violating the laws of Nature in asking the Poor to alter their lives so as to protect them in the future from poverty. He knew less about Natural laws than the social laws under which he himself principally lived. To him, what he asked of the Poor seemed very easy. He took a bath every morning ; but it was a domestic who prepared the bath for him on the previous nights. He was very liberal in the matter of towels, because he was a great believer in friction ; but then it was his laundry, either public or private, that washed and prepared his towels for him. He went to his linen-drawer while dressing, and found there all he wanted in the way of shirts, collars, cuffs. He threw them off whenever he wished to, and saw them no more until they were nestling again amidst their spotless brethren waiting their turn. After this fashion personal cleanliness was very easy ; but how much of the labour of it in his case was due to the philanthropist himself? The workman, if he had a bath, would require to attend to it himself. He would be too tired in the evening, and have no time in the morning. His wife would have to wash his towels, and she has no time. And having no laundry, when he wears clean linen it is at half a day's expense of somebody hanging over the washtub. It is astonishing how little of the routine of our lives we do for ourselves, and how much of it is done for us by others ; and in those things we are in the habit of saying " I do " and " I did " we are oftener nearer the mark if we said we permitted them to be done to us. If we were as the Poor, and had to do everything for ourselves, with how little we could put up ! Ask the miner, and the camper-out generally. Or if we determined to try single-handed how much we

could do in a day, the result would be too disappointing
to attempt to keep up with the demands of social life
as long as we remained unaided. But the better class
know no other life than that of being done for, and at
that cost the result is very satisfactory ; and when the
Poor refused both their advice and example, because
they would require to do everything for themselves, the
philanthropists were very angry.

It was indifference, they said—indifference to their
own well-being, indifference to their own comfort, and,
worst ingratitude of all, indifference to the labours, the
advice, and wishes of those who were working for their
good.

When a person, man or woman, starts philanthro-
pising, it is not a trifle that can stop them : certainly
that reason which less prejudiced people would think
should be final and all-sufficient, has in the past, and
even in the present day, little effect upon them—that is,
that their services are neither desired nor necessary.
The indifference of the Poor was not to be allowed to
stand in the way of their improvement—we must, said
the philanthropist, rouse them from their indifference.
Many ways were tried, all more or less based upon
bribery, and, as we have said, the poor took the bribes
and continued in their old way as before. Then the
philanthropists discovered an *awful fact*—the poor remained in their own form of life, with all its occasional
hardships, because they were happier that way, they
believed, than in the brand-new moral and sober life
offered to them by their reformers !

This knowledge to any other persons than reformers
would have shown them their mistake. They had come
there with the happiness of the Poor at heart. It was
to increase that happiness for which, they declared,
they laboured ; and finding that the present form of
life of the Poor was a happier one than any they could

offer, there was nothing for them to do but admit their
error and retire : or if they were really single-minded
in their desire for the happiness of the Poor, they should
have made their life the subject of their studies, and
tried to alter the worser parts by such infinitesimal
degrees that the Poor would hardly feel the change,
would, in fact, drop into the alteration naturally as by
gravitation.   But philanthropists soon become more
enamoured of their specific than the people it is meant
to benefit.   It is so common, it might almost be called
the rule, that philanthropists who interest themselves in
a class, from a sympathetic affection to do them good,
become ere long their most cordial haters—crime : they
will not dance to the philanthropist's piping.   Such
was the case with the old philanthropists in this
instance.   They were angry that the Poor should be
so happy in their misery.   It was intolerable, after
they had laboured so long to make them happy in
another way.   The philanthropist is never in error,
and between the two lives there could be no comparison as to which was the truly happy one.   The
happiness of the Poor must be destroyed so that the
newer life may become attractive.   When we destroy a
person's happiness, and reduce him to a state of abject
misery, a life of few attractions becomes even desirable.
If these good and well-intentioned people had had parliamentary power, as they desired to have, they would
have destroyed the homes and household gods of the
Poor.   They would have forbidden their habits, taken
charge of their expenditure, banished their amusements, and turned their hours of leisure into a drill-
ground of religion, hygiene, and education.   They
would have made the Poor as unhappy as legislation
could make them, in the hope that the virtuous but
unlovely life of reform they offered them might become
attractive.   They had no legal powers, so they deter-

mined to try what powers they had, they determined to
preach to the poor the Gospel of Discontent.

Nothing seems stranger than to look back a few
years and see hundreds of good and pious people
earnestly engaged on a hundred platforms in attempting
to destroy the happiness of a large section of their
fellow-men. Invective, sarcasm, ridicule, indignation,
and contempt were all employed in their exhortations
to the Poor to give up their happiness. Were they
going to live like the brutes? Were they going to
stagnate and rot? Were they going to be for ever
content with their sty, like the swine? Was their
whole aim in life to be meat for the belly and clothes
for the back, then a folding of hands, and sleep? Was
to-morrow and to-morrow to be as this day till life
ended? All these and many other sayings were hurled
at the workman to make him miserable. Every step
he took seemed to bring a new and special curse into
his ears. He was told to rouse himself, and shake off
his sloth. He was to put aside all his own likes and
indulgences. He was to struggle for a larger house ;
he was to be better clothed ; his family were to be
better educated and better fed ; his wife's vanity was
to be allowed a larger indulgence in the way of finery
(it was not so stated ; it was put that his wife should
have an opportunity of being more respectable), and
his evenings were to be spent in self-improvement.
Such a change of text did not add popularity to the
mission, and indeed it was strange to see the few who
were bribed and coaxed to attend coming out from
one of the meetings with a cold shiver running down
their backs, their hearts in their boots, and their
capacity for any kind of enjoyment that night totally
destroyed. At the meetings they no more heard of
the joys of heaven, they sang no hymns of the Better
Land. They had been stormed at, their habits and

ways denounced from their rising in the morning to their rest. They were to be made miserable, and they felt it.

All this did little good to the mission because few went near it. The philanthropist was never wise in his or any generation. Not having legal power to make the old life impossible, to make it unhappy did not make a virtuous life attractive. It made the old life more attractive. To drive a dog away from a bone does not make a biscuit more attractive to him while the bone still remains in sight. The Poor might be made temporarily unhappy by the reformer's denunciations, but when these passed away it was the old life to which they clung. A cordial hatred of the mission, missionaries, and philanthropists sprung up among the Poor as a reward for their exertions, and the philanthropists sighed and fumed alternately that they were without power.

At last the power came; but not to the philanthropist: to the workman. What wonder, then, that the workman should use his new powers to demand that better condition of life that had been preached at him in season and out of season as absolutely necessary both to his health and morals, and that his wages were unable to furnish! How could the philanthropists resist such a demand? It was themselves who had taught it. The gist of their whole argument, whether they spoke on behalf of religion, morality, or education was that these virtues were a mere matter of money. By saving his money and directing it to certain objects the wage-earner might become virtuous, but not otherwise; and each particular virtue demanded a larger tribute from his wages than they could afford. Religion demanded of him respectability, and among the poor respectability means clothes. It is one of the glaring hypocrisies of the Church, that it welcomes the Poor without distinction of garment. Religion is nothing if not outwardly respectable. Let the workman in his oily or his limy clothes appear at the mission, and it is all right for the first night. Let him come again the same way, and he gets worried to death to come respectable, and if he cannot procure the clothes, the mission will. Respectability meant a duplication of the clothes of himself and family; a capital expenditure far beyond his means. Morality taught him that there could be no virtue, chastity, or sexual purity unless the sexes lived apart. The workman, the poorer sort, who occupied a house of one apartment, found to be moral he would require to double his rent and take a house of two apartments, an expenditure he did not feel called upon to cope with. He was not much interested in morality: he left that to the women folks, believing it was a matter more of their affairs than his. He lived as his grandfather and great-grandfather had lived before him from time immemorial, and their women folks knew how to protect themselves. Their minds did not run so perpetually upon the immoral as their wealthier sisters, and so they could enjoy a greater scope of freedom with innocence. The educationist (before the School Board days) told him that all depravity arose from a want of an adequate knowledge of the three Rs. At the same time, that knowledge had to be bought and paid for in hard cash; and when the Sanitarian came along, *his* requirements showed the workman that double his wages, all his spare time, and an incessant strain of attention would hardly be sufficient to meet them. The summing-up of all these arguments was, in the minds of the Poor, that a man with only twenty shillings a week could not be moral, whereas a skilled workman or a small trader with two pounds to two pounds ten shillings a week could not be otherwise, as he had all the requirements in clothes, houses, and means of education in which virtue resided. The Poor had many songs and stories of the olden time in which all virtue was depicted as purely personal qualities as partial to the dwellers in the hut as in the palace. Some poets went further, and believed the lowly cot a better seedplot of virtue than the court of princes. But the Poor also knew there was a great change coming over the spirit of the age, and that money was now becoming everything ; and so perhaps virtue was falling under its potent influence also. But the strange thing remained, that it was not said that money could buy virtue, but that, like the tea-men who push their sales by giving presents with the purchases, it was given away to people of a certain income, an income un-fortunately a good deal larger than theirs.

We do not say there is a connecting link directly associating the philanthropists' Gospel of Discontent and the socialist agitators' demands. But there is this strange coincidence, that for the first time in the history of industrial labour in this country the Poor were being taught that virtue was largely a matter of income. At the same time they received the franchise, and the first articulate demand the socialists among them made was for an income commensurate with the practice of virtue independent of all economic conditions, that their arguments were an exact repetition of the arguments of the philanthropists ; that the only people who sup-ported them in their preposterous demands were the wealthy philanthropists and their friends ; and that the term a "living wage," so common in our ears since, meant when first used a moral or virtuous living wage, i.e., a wage sufficient to let the workmen live a moral or virtuous life according to the scale laid down by the philanthropist.

There is a proverb that it is only the first step that is

difficult, and certainly in socialism after the first step it is remarkably easy, and from the "living wage" of only a few years ago they have progressed in their demands, the latest being—only as a temporary expedient until they take everything in the shape of wealth—that wages should never be reduced; that they should have thirty shillings a week when doing what theatrical folk call "resting"; that a grateful country should afford them every attention and luxury during sickness or accident; and that they should retire upon an ample pension at the extreme old age of fifty. When that state of affairs comes about, the philanthropist must think—how very virtuous the people will become!

CHAPTER VI

A CHAPTER OF ADVICE: INDIVIDUALITY, HABIT,
IMITATION.

A chapter of advice—The Natural laws of Individuality, Habit,
and Imitation as they affect the lives of the Poor.

In the cosmogony of Nature all life was individual,
absolutely and integrally a separate entity from all
the rest of the world : a perfect machine giving and
receiving no aid from any other form of life. Each life
had its destiny, and the proper functions to try and
attain it ; and although that destiny was the common
destiny of all life, to it, it was the destiny of itself only ;
it could not interpret the aims or feelings of any other
living thing, and life to it only existed in and for itself.
We see that form of life still in the vegetable world.
Each blade of grass, though there be millions in a
field, is as independent as if it grew alone. It requires
nothing of any other blade of grass. The vigorous
may destroy the weaker, may take the sun from some ;
but at the same time may be protecting others from the
wind's rough blast. Yet they are neither cruel nor
kind : they have not turned aside to do these things.
They are pursuing their destiny, for which purpose life
was given them. There are no theories of mutual

G

helpfulness, no communism or socialism in the vegetable world, because there are none needing help.

When we come to the animal kingdom we find a different state of things. Degeneracy has here set in, and has gone too far for us to guess what was the primal strength of the various kinds, and how far we have fallen from it. But there is a science by which wise men trace back the history of animal life from rudimentary remains, and if we follow that plan we may find we have still some of our primal Natural laws amongst us, although we have long since lost the faculties they governed.

The first noticeable point is that the wildest animals are still the strongest, and we may presume are nearer to their original nature. When we speak of strength we do not mean mere muscularity, but that perfect proportion of power in an animal that for offensive and defensive purposes makes it fearless, and independent to follow its habits. The elephant may be more muscular than the lion, tiger, or leopard, but it is not so strong. It herds together sometimes, showing a weakness in defensive qualities. The whale may be larger and more muscular than the shark, but it is not so strong, because it " schools," showing that numbers are necessary to the protection of the individual. The predatory animals are generally found alone ; they require nothing of any other animal, and they can do their business best by themselves. Next in strength come the animals that herd, the birds that flock, the fish that shoal. These reserve their individuality in all things but the one weak and common object that keeps them together-- it may be for defence, it may be for direction ; but whatever it is for, it is a weakness, a falling away from original strength that can only be covered by numbers. To require the assistance of anything or anybody is a confession of personal weakness ;

and that we feel it a defect, we not only are continually rebelling against it, but we see that the young in their extra vigour and energy are always less gregarious than the old, more independent because of their strength. But the most degenerate form of all life is the form that has been reduced to combination and co-operation, such as the bee, the ant, the beaver. The deer may herd with the deer from youth to old age, and neither would ever give the other a drink, would save fodder for it, would help it if it were wounded. All that they ask of each other is the strength of their presence, the aid of their watchfulness. But such animals and insects that have become so weak that they have lost the power of doing certain things for themselves, and are dependent for these things on others, have reached the lowest stage of life ; rather half-life or quarter-life, as they cannot live without the other half or three-quarters that make the complement of their hive or colony.

The next rudimentary law still effective in animal life by which we may guess their relative degeneracy is their inclination or disinclination to motion. The destiny of life is rest : happiness is rest ; and the stillest forms of life are the strongest and nearest original conditions. The predatory animals are almost never in motion unless when hunting. All the animals that work singly only work from the compulsion of necessity. Nature is incapable of a single unnecessary action. Strength has two special qualities always at work, the one the power to satisfy all its desires, the other the power to suppress all unnatural and unattainable desires. Weakness, on the other hand, does not restrict and limit its desires to within its own powers of accomplishment. Its desires increase in proportion as it is unable to attain them. The solitary working animals, having all their life and functions, their aims and objects, within themselves, exhibit the perfection of achievement. The herding and flocking animals have to surrender part of their individuality for the protection they receive; they are therefore more on the motion to keep with the company. They cannot rest when they wish, or linger where they wish, as the stronger animals can. They must be with the herd, and rest when it rests. There is much personal labour entailed upon the herding and flocking animals and birds, because of the weakness that binds them together. Nature has its law of "equivalents," and for the benefit of communion, individuality must in proportion be surrendered. Individuality is the most essential quality we possess for the maintenance and conservation of personal strength, and its surrender is a greater loss than any gain we can derive from combination.

The co-operative forms of life have almost wholly lost their individuality. They cannot rest when they wish; they cannot change their minds under changing circumstances; they have no liberty to be swayed by any new or attractive events; they must do their share of the mutual work. Under the impulse of hunger the tiger may start out on the hunt, but may be drawn away by some counter attraction. It has no other animal to consult on the matter; and if the new attraction rises higher in interest to the tiger than its hunger it most certainly will follow it. Not so the poor ant; its life is not its own, it belongs to its community. It is a slave among slaves for the pleasure of existence. It dare not economise its labour, because that is due to others: it is needless for it to economise its consumption, because that is provided by others. It represents the maximum of labour and the minimum of rest. Yet rest is happiness, labour is pain.

All weaker forms of life are of a more intricate construction, a more complex organisation. Nature made

all things strong and simple ; but in the degeneracy
of life, and the feeling of waning strength, the individual form had to begin within itself the process of
combination and organisation. What had originally
been accomplished by one or two simple functions had
to have special organs developed to attend to each separ-
ately ; and this subdivision went on as each new crisis
of exhausted energy threatened to engulf the whole life.
As combination with others demanded a surrender of
individuality, so the multiplication of separate organs in
the body destroyed the autonomy of the whole. Each
of these organs could get out of order from causes
affecting itself only—that is, independently and by
itself—and thereby disarrange the whole machinery.
Each could contract disease by itself that could kill
the whole organism. The machinery that was to
benefit by having so many sections never knew when
it might be stopped by one or other of these sections
getting out of order. Wise and skilled mechanics
never admire or approve of complicated machinery ;
yet we are taught to believe that the complexity and
delicacy of the human organism is a special sign of
man's superiority. That is one of the peculiar forms
of man's vanity. Without caring to inquire too curi-
ously into the truth that might be disagreeable to him,
he has adopted the rule that wherever he differs from
the other forms of animal creation the difference is
always an evidence of his superiority. Reader, if you
are at any time asked to admire the wonders of Providence, or the beauties of Nature in some fine and
delicate organism, some complex form of life, some
manifold arrangement of functions in the same animal,
and besought to believe they are higher, superior
objects of creation, read your history aright, and see
only in those weak and fragile objects evidences of the
degeneracy of life, every function and every organ

being the milestones that mark its descent from pristine strength and simplicity.

Nature has a law within all forms of life, called the Economy of Effort, that refuses to allow it to use any more energy in any action than what is known or found to be necessary. The animals, &c., that combine and co-operate know this. They know that nothing but necessity has driven them to surrender their individuality and freedom. The animal that has a member or an organ more than another does not feel itself to be of a higher order of creation thereby, but thinks sadly of the time when some weak progenitor was forced to add this further burden to his armour, that his descendants must use and waste energy over, perhaps for all time. These animals, though forced to combine and co-operate, do not extend their operations in that direction; the law of individuality works steadily in them, keeping them seeking and dreaming for the strength that would give them independence.

What position man occupies in this sliding-scale of life it would take up too much space to describe. His case is peculiar. Into his life have passed vicissitudes and episodes that so far as we know, all other forms of life have avoided. Some of these have hastened the decay; some have arrested it, and for a time invigorated the weak and nerveless constitution; others, again, have been unequal in their action, strengthening some at the expense of others. His strong desire for independence in his own person, but uniformity in others, has kept him nursing his individuality, that in many cases it appears so strong as to give one the impression that its strength is unimpaired, and this individuality makes it impossible for him to combine to any great extent, either in numbers or duration. There is so great diversity found within the race that in some aspects it may be taken as a microcosm of the whole life-world.

To the great mechanical and methodical subdivisions of labour we see around us, such as the management of railways, the building of ships, &c., we make no allusion here. To do these things men have to be trained, and to what men are trained is not Natural. These are only indications how highly men can be trained for money, and sometimes the man capable of the highest training for co-operating in this form may be so strongly individual as to have almost no social cohesion with his fellow-men. When we take Natural actions in man we will see how little power of combination he has. In the face of national or common danger he combines as well as the other animals. While the danger is imminent, there is no talk of precedence, no quarrels of leaders, no divided counsels. Then none are for a party, all are for the State. But remove the danger, sufficient to give them breathing time, delay it long enough for them to get past their apprehension, and their individuality asserts itself, and disaffection and disintegration set in. Rebellion against oppression we know to be a plant of very slow growth. The individual sufferer at the moment is all for rebellion, but those who are not suffering, find their individual interests rise higher than the common one, and the general history of rebellions is, that while fortune smiles upon them they are supported, and *vice versa*. So much of all forms of combinations of men is governed by authority in civilized countries that little is left to individualism. This is the best proof of man's incapacity to combine. Nothing but some power greater than and above himself can hold him in action or interest with his fellow-man. Thieves, we know, fall out over the division of the spoil. They risk long terms of imprisonment in gaining it, and then betray each other in their bitter or noisy quarrelling over its distribution. This common occurrence is known to kings as well as criminals.

All the Natural laws in man are ministers to his individuality. Although he has cultivated the habit of sociability, it, too, is dominated by individualism. When a man finds any circle unprofitable to him, he leaves it, and seeks another more congenial. He alone knows what he seeks from society and if he finds it ; nor is he sure that for two successive days it will be the same thing.

The habits of the Poor of the present day are the product of centuries, centuries during which they had only one object, that of finding their happiness. Their present mode of life is the highest attainment of pleasure at the least expenditure of money and effort. They have had to work out the problem against environment, the conditions of labour, natural disadvantages, and the laws of the land, and no human being but one of themselves could improve upon it. And even one of themselves could only affect it in some trifling detail. Yet it changes constantly, but slowly, and imperceptibly to the livers, but seeable in periods of time by the historian and observer. Slowly as it changes it can neither be forced nor arrested.

The forces at work in changing the habits of the Poor and all other classes are two—exhaustion and imitation. Civilisation having destroyed the natural instinct in man whereby he knew all things that came within the limits of his interests, whether they would be useful or otherwise, or, in other words, the instinct of selection, he has to acquire the knowledge by imitation. To a small extent we are influenced by education, because education is thrust upon us ; but it is always over-ridden by imitation, because education is disagreeable and artificial and insincere in the teacher. We do not imitate disagreeable things ;

we are seeking our happiness, and, having to depend upon our fellow-man for our knowledge of pleasure, we only imitate him in what he seems to enjoy, in what he is in earnest in, his natural, and perhaps unconscious, expression in all moods. The Poor do not copy the virtues of the better classes, because the better classes do not show any happiness in their virtues, and are fools enough to tell the Poor that there is no happiness but that of religious duty found in them. But the Poor are quite willing to imitate the pleasures of the Rich, if they have the means. The child who knows every inflexion of her mother's voice, and every emotion they betray, knows perfectly well that when her mother assumes an artificial tone never used on any other occasion, and stilted formal language that bears no relation to her natural conversation, that she is neither natural nor happy. She may be teaching the child a prayer, or improving her morals ; all the child knows is that the whole thing is depressing and unreal. She has therefore no desire to imitate such moods. See the same child an hour or so afterwards, with wide open eyes and intense expression, listening to her mother scolding the servant, or deep in gossip with a visitor. Then she knows the parties are in earnest, and in the latter case enjoying themselves. So she gets her doll and scolds it in the language of her mother, or makes a gossip of it to talk scandal. The untutored native sees nothing of happiness in the life or teaching of the Missionary. (Often the poor missionary sees little himself.) The savage might wish to have his coat or waistcoat because he sees the missionary attaches a mysterious importance to his garments, and the nigger might wish to know what virtue is in them. But see the difference when the trader comes along. With open eyes the nigger sees how masterful he is. Whether it is cattle or bearers he has, see how he manages them ; hear his oaths. Then he smokes tobacco and drinks spirits, and no man can doubt the expression he wears of contentment and satisfaction over these operations. There, there is something for imitation if you will, and the nigger will have learned the whole contents of a slang dictionary, ere he can repeat the Lord's Prayer.

Because our habits are imitative and not natural to us, we tire of them ; we exhaust them ; we find them out. They become insufficient for our purpose, and we drop them, to pick up others. The other animals and birds having retained their instinct of selection, choose habits exactly suited to their needs, and never change them. They have the same satisfying power last as first. The process of exchanging our habits, we have said, is slow and imperceptible, because they are generally changed one at a time, and a man may have a hundred actions in his day, all interwoven with each other, all interdependent upon each other for the pleasure they bring, and when one is being discarded its tendons have to be gently unravelled and released from the others, without pain or disturbance. And the new one has to be slowly grafted on in like cautious manner.

The Natural law of the exchange of habit is to acquire a more restful, less active habit than the discarded one, if possible—what the moral people call slothful and of downward tendency. But it is in obedience to the two fundamental laws in us, Rest and the Economy of Effort, and it matters not whether it be called upwards, downwards, or crossways, it is onward to Rest and Strength. The social law of habit is the opposite ; by it habits are chosen because of their expensiveness and labour, in the hope that our social rival may be discomfited, and unable to follow us. From this social rivalry comes the great energy of habit of our social classes, and it is these vigorous habits they extol so much as virtues ; habits in reality the product of petty rivalries. In the better classes are the same Natural laws as in the Poor, the desire for Rest and the Economy of Effort, but they are suppressed for the sake of social distinction, and tiresome, laborious habits adopted. No wonder they tire of them so quickly. There is nothing in them but their selectness, and when that goes they go also.

But the Poor are more natural than the Rich, and their habits endure longer. Yet how strange it seems to the Poor for people to come among them and tell them that virtue, and presumably happiness, lies in toiling when there is no need for it. All virtues are laborious.

Again, the habits of the classes are toilsome and expensive, according to their means, but the labour does not fall upon the people who enjoy them ; nor even then would the habit be very enjoyable if it were not supported by everything that can contribute to heighten its pleasure : servants, houses, carriages, leisure, &c. Stripped of their accessories, the most of them would be intolerable ; yet the philanthropists recommend these to the Poor, who must take them bare if they take them at all.

Associated with the desire to improve the conditions of life of the Poor is the hope (but fond delusion) that the Poor will cultivate the virtues common to the people who enjoy the intended improvements already, and some go even further (parsons especially) and are confidently expecting a development of morality greater than exists at present in the standard of improvement they are to attain. How such a thing is to come about it is difficult to imagine, more especially with the strong tendency in the Poor to descend in the social or laborious scale, rather than ascend. There exists at present, or has existed, in various parts of the country cases where the Poor have enjoyed all the improvements it is possible to offer them, and their use of these advantages is patent to all but the bat-like philanthropist, who refuses to have his sentiments disturbed by the intrusion of facts.

In certain districts of the country there are colliers who have enjoyed shorter hours of labour than the much-cried-for eight, and who only work five days in the week as a rule, and sometimes only four. Does the advantage of so much daily leisure incline them to literary tastes? Such a question would be laughed at by any one of themselves if put to him. Beyond the evening papers with the " odds " in it, they seek no more literature. The extra time allows them to elaborate their pleasures, gives them opportunities of enjoying more exciting amusements. And elaborate pleasures and strong excitement is in the eyes of the philanthropist more immoral than those they could enjoy if they had only an hour or two between their work and their bed. Nor is this in country districts where the workmen have no libraries, no conveniences for reading and study. In some cases the pits are within the boundaries of the town ; the men live in the town, and the town has public libraries, art galleries, &c. But of this latter fact, not one in five of the workmen is aware, not one in fifty cares, and not one in a hundred will ever put their foot within them.

There are free libraries and museums, and, but more rarely, art galleries scattered over many of the towns in England and Scotland that the workmen never put a foot into. The student, the country lodger, and such like are their only visitors, and in many cases it is not for mental improvement, but to pass the time.

There are gymnasia in many towns that have been presented by public-spirited citizens, who have imagined the working classes have been sighing for such a form

of amusement. There has been the usual presentation
by the donor, and speech by the mayor accepting the
gift on behalf of the town, and an oration by a professor upon athletics, and then the usual adjournment
to the banquet-hall for cake and wine. For the first
week extra police are required at the gymnasium to
keep order. The thing is new, and many want to see
it. Six months afterwards, the chains are dangling in
rust, the ladders are rungless, the trusses are all cut
into with initials, swings are broken, &c. Nobody is
ever seen to amuse himself in it but a few boys, and
the idle take possession of it to destroy it. So is it also
with fountains, statues, and all ornamental work put
among the Poor to educate them. When not abused,
they are treated with indifference. Nobody wants
them ; nobody cares for them. The people go past
them and around them, sit sometimes at the base of the
statues, or in the chairs surrounding the fountains, and
never give a thought what they are.

There have been hundreds of instances where poor
workmen have got the offer of larger houses than they
chose to pay for, either rent free or at a nominal rent.
We have known many cases. These houses were
generally old houses within works, that the proprietors
had not made up their minds what to do with, whether
to add them to the works or pull them down altogether.
On the principle that a house is kept in better condition
when inhabited than when empty, they offer them
temporarily to some poor, deserving workman. In
other cases they are cottages in connection with large
works that cover a great area. The cottage overlooks,
perhaps, some unguarded part. It is cheaper to give
the cottage to a workman than to pay a watchman.
A poor workman with a family is selected, because the
family will always be about the door as a look-out.
How then do the Poor take advantage of these offers?

They bring their few sticks of furniture from their old
house ; they do not, nor would they, spend one farthing
on the further furnishing of their house. So far as the
furniture will cover, they cover, and they live exactly
as in the previous house to the extent of their furnishing.
All the rest is left empty and bare, where the children
can play themselves, and the mother make a drying-
green of on a wet day. But where it is permitted, or
where it can be done under the rose, they invariably let
the empty space to lodgers : young, strong labourers
who have next to no belongings, and do not care where
they sleep, their principal concern being where they
will get breakfast. For these, the daughters are turned
out of their bed and given a shakedown on the floor of
one of the rooms. Where is the great moral influence
of the separation of the sexes to flow from in these
cases ? There are no locked doors, sometimes not even
shut ones. There is too much traffic in and out all
evening, and until very late they do not know for certain
how many guests they may have. They go to sleep at
all hours, some early, some late, and they roam about
with perfect freedom, none daring to be so exclusive as
to appropriate any more space than he or she can lie
upon.

What about the morals ? What about the sanitation
that the better housing of the Poor was to stimulate ?

These being individual cases may be felt to be insufficient. Let us take, then, an instance with which
every citizen of an ordinary sized town is acquainted
with. Every town has its slums. Who make these
slums ? Not the natural decay of properties ; not the
desertion of the fashionable people from the neighbourhood ; not the rapacious landlord rack-renting the Poor
in his insanitary dwelling. None of these. The Poor
make the slums for their own convenience. In the
making of slums, that the Poor should take advantage

of a deserted neighbourhood is only saying that, like everybody else, they profit by whatever opportunities present themselves. But they will make slums if there be no deserted localities. The decay of property is often the result of slum life, rather than the inducement. The Poor make slums of quite new property. And the idea that any landlord can invite the Poor to become his tenants in an insanitary building at a higher rent than they choose to pay, is one of the greatest fallacies that has ever been circulated by the ignorant, credulous philanthropist. Of all people in the world how can the Poor in cities be rack-rented? They have virtually no furniture; their rents are collected weekly in advance; there is nothing to keep them from removing on a few hours' notice. Those who cannot pay have to go, and are accustomed to shifting, but in that case they have to live with friends until their finances are restored. The general plan is to coax and wheedle the landlord to give them time, and curse him heartily when his patience is exhausted. There are slump-rents at all prices, and there is nothing to induce a man to pay more than he chooses. On the other hand, the landlord has no weapon to protect his property from being made slum-property but by raising his rents; and once a property is "slummed" it is ruined. And when a property has been "slummed" raising the rent is the only recourse the owner has for the removal of objectionable and suspicious characters. His tenants are too many, and the rents too small to indulge in legal forms.

There are some cities philanthropically inclined who acquired power to tear down their slums. They were a godsend to the proprietors of that kind of property, who got a very good price for their buildings, and were in the main glad to be rid of them. But the displaced

Poor were the people who suffered most, and the shop-men who depended upon their trade, next. The former had to go and form new rookeries, often to the land-lord's disgust, and the latter had to remove also, or become bankrupt when there was no population to trade with. The process of forming a slum is very simple—we have seen it often. One of the slummers has only to take an empty house in any of the pro-perties in the locality they have chosen as their own. The house may be larger, and the rent dearer than he is inclined to pay, but he sublets parts of it, and fills the rest with lodgers. Complaint is made to the land-lord, but ere he can take legal steps, the other tenants have fled. No tenant, with a little furniture, a steady wage, and an attempt at respectability, will endure the reproach of living among slummers. The landlord can never rehabilitate his property. He has the choice of keeping it empty, or filling it with the Poor, and when he chooses the latter, they swarm in like bees. While they are doing so the neighbours on both sides are flying from the spot, and new tenements are ready for the Poor as fast as they can fill them. The philanthro-pists of the City Improvement schemes seemed to have a notion that when they had torn down rookeries, straightened and widened streets, that the remaining space would be eagerly leased by the builder to erect new and improved buildings. But having driven the Poor away to other quarters, when they were ready to lease their ground there were no inhabitants; nothing but dreary wastes of ruins and hoardings without trade or life. Under no circumstances could the old inhabit-ants be conjured back to the locality, and until a new class found some use for these barren spots they remained deserts in the heart of the city.

There are some societies formed for the better housing of the Poor. The people who form these

societies might as well take for their object the providing of drier atmosphere for fish.   Some have built
new buildings, some have bought old buildings and
repaired and improved them up to the latest sanitary
standard.   The houses have high ceilings, the necessary
amount of light and cubic space to each apartment,
and all sanitary conveniences, and in some cases they
have added inside fixtures to which the ordinary classes
are   accustomed,   but   the   Poor   are   not.   These
fixtures can easily be destroyed, or unfixed and carried
away.

To get bank interest for the money invested they
require to charge a rent the Poor will never be inclined
to   pay.   To   protect   their   property   they   require
" decent " tenants, and it is to escape respectability
that the Poor form their slums.   To do a lot of
cleaning, &c., which they know the Poor would never
do themselves, they have a resident janitor or care-
taker, and the Poor will never submit to such espionage.
Who, then, fill these houses, because they get rapidly
filled ?   A better class come down to them.   People
who have been paying more rent for larger houses.
The newly-built houses have architectural pretensions
and broad pavements, with large well-lighted shops on
the ground floor : the bought and improved houses
have been made respectable by the alterations and the
selection of tenants.   This is a lower standard of
respectability than existed before, and those who had
to pay for more than they wanted are glad of the
opportunity to save their rent.   Thus these philanthropists are helping the Natural law of descent by
providing people with smaller and cheaper houses than
they were content with before.

The slum is as necessary to the Poor as the palace
to the Rich.   The poor man does not live in his house
as the better classes do ; he lives on the street, and

only uses his house as a retreat for food or rest.
Requiring no more than that, he is not going to pay
much rent for it. He is not going to keep curtains in
his window, or polish the handle of his door. He is
going to have no rivalries about cleanest houses, or
finest furniture. All these things belong to people
who live in their houses. He lives on the street. The
street is his home. There he meets his friends ; there
he is known ; there he finds his amusements ; there is
his favourite public-house ; there is his reading-room,
news-room, and art gallery. It is for his street he
pays the price of a good rent in cars to take him to
his work and back at night ; it is for his street that he
pays the landlord the high rent which he does. His
attachment is to his street ; not his house.

So far as we have seen from experience, no moral
improvement may be expected from any improvement
of the material condition of the Poor, unless it is one
that they themselves desire, one that is a hindrance in
the meantime to the free play of their virtuous instincts.
What such hindrances are, we will deal with by and
by, but as they almost all arise from the difference in the
standards of morality of the two classes, so they can
be removed by an assimilation of these standards into
a working law of life for all humanity.

CHAPTER VII

LABOUR

Labour the penalty of life—The evolution of the wage-earner—
The effect of machinery : to make labour a caste—Limits of
the workman's ambition circumscribed—Strikes—Municipal
workshops—A suggestion for the utilisation of the unemployed.

LABOUR is the curse of human existence, made so by
man—a curse from which every man, woman, and
child that was ever born into the world, or ever will
be, has fled from, and will flee from, as from a pesti-
lence. The busiest person engaged in physical labour,
if his actions are free, only shows the eager desire with
which he is anticipating, or seeking to anticipate, his
emancipation. The Poor will sweat and toil to give
their children better education and better clothing than
their position allows, in their endeavour to get them
into situations where they can escape physical labour.
And these same children will accept gladly a lower
wage than they could otherwise earn, with greater
demands upon it, making their lives one long strain
of the severest repression, to escape the hated thing.
The man of small or straitened means, blessed with
a family of daughters, will submit to almost any form

of retrenchment to save his girls from going out. That
is the irretrievable step in social distinction. They may
be clever, well-educated, well-trained young ladies;
no personal charm or qualification can compensate
for such a fatal action. The ill-bred, under-educated,
under-mannered daughter of a successful tradesman
is aware of her social superiority to the lady who may
have to go out, and will have no hesitation in reminding the latter of the difference between them. The
merchant may receive a legacy, and he puts it into
his business for further speculation; the tradesman
may become heir to some money, and his first thoughts
are upon extending his business; but the workman's
one hope of succeeding to money is to quit labour.
Young or middle-aged, no matter how easy or well
paid, if man can live without labour nothing will
induce him to work.

Why labour is so repulsive to man is because it is
unnatural. Nature's order of toil is as follows. All
living things must find the material for their existence
from the earth. Water and food was all that was
required, nor could they seek for these until Nature
within them called for them; thus what "work" was
required of them was sought for under a stimulus that
made their labour so light they did not feel it. The
pangs of hunger or of thirst possessed them to the
exclusion of any knowledge of their labour to appease
them. But, further, lest any animal or bird should
take a liking for work of any kind, unless under the
inspiration of immediate want, Nature implanted in all
of her creations a law which prohibits them from any
unnecessary motion. This was Nature's plan to keep
all things from disturbing her order and arrangement
of the earth. But man, who came to believe the earth
was made for him, changed all this.

When authority was discovered by man it produced

slavery, and as slavery permitted those in authority to
escape even Nature's limit of personal labour, it was
very welcome. Happiness is rest. A wave of slavery
passed all over the known world, and from this slavery
civilisation sprung. No number of men could be found
anywhere with sufficient cohesion to form a " nation "
without the strong coercing the weak. No ancient
city ever was built by freemen ; no king, or nation, or
contractor had money enough to pay their wages.
They were all built by slaves, working under the lash
—driven, stalled, and fed like other beasts of burden.
In the slave all Natural laws were driven away, and the
hours of his labour were the ascertained power of endurance in him. This did not alter the nature of man,
but intensified his hatred of labour and his love of
freedom. The only good point of slavery was that it
destroyed poverty. The most prolific source of poverty
is, not that a man cannot feed himself from his labours,
but that he will not. The slave got no choice in the
matter ; the reward of his labour was his keep, and in
the interests of his master it was seen to that he was
fed. If the slave had been given money to buy his
food, he would have spent as much of it as he dared
on other pleasures. If he could, he would have sold
his food and clothing for something he longed for,
something he envied others the enjoyment of. But
the master required a strong, well-fed, healthy slave,
and their feeding he had to see to himself.

Here was the first difference of interests between
employer and employed, a difference that, having
remained unsolved all these years, is as acute to-day
as ever. The employer, and you, the philanthropist—
as you belong to the employer class you also hold his
opinions—believe that the first use a workman should
put his wages to is to provide " the necessaries of life "
for himself and family ; while the workman, though

not holding any opinion on the matter, uniformly acts
as if the family bread-and-butter was his very last consideration—as it generally is. A thing of daily occurrence cannot rise to be a matter of consuming interest
unless something uncommon happens to it ; and it is
only when he is compelled to give the matter his attention that the workman thinks about the condition of his
larder. Even then, it is made the scapegoat for all
shortages or retrenchments. When the workman is
animated with a strong desire for something, the purchase of which will make such inroads upon his pay
that he will be obliged to live for the week on very
short commons, his belief in how little food he can live
upon is marvellous. The question is only relatively
one of poverty ; it is more directly one of wages. If
the workman were first to provide the needs of his
household, even on a generous scale, it would soon
become known what the average cost of living was,
and how much the workman had remaining at his free
disposal. This would be very pleasant to the philanthropist and society in general, because it would produce
in the workman a more regular and steady mode of life.
To the employer it would also be very grateful, as he
would make that remainder balance the Aunt Sally
of every wave of depression or bad market he had. As
long as the employer believed the workman had a
balance, he would consider the latter overpaid. The
employer believes that the workman works for a
living. Not so the workman. He knows what he
works for : he works for the pleasure of spending his
wages as he thinks fit. He has got rid of the last
vestiges of the Truck Acts—useful, beneficial acts for
the reduction of poverty, but scandalously abused by
the greed of the employers ; he has got rid of everything that comes between him and hard cash for every
penny of his wages ; and how he chooses to dispose

of them he considers his own affair. But we know it is the smallest portion that goes towards household expenses ; and if that small proportion is not enough, then he complains that his whole wages are insufficient to support him and his family, and he is ready for a strike. If lowness of wages had any bearing upon the poverty of the working classes, it would be worth inquiring here what a minimum wage should be ; but so little has it to do with the question, that when from any cause the workman's wages cease, it is the higher paid who are first in distress. This is because they live on a higher plane than the others. They become used to regular meals and full meals, and a suspension of these brings them to unendurable distress at once, while their more frugal neighbours (compulsorily so) eat at irregular times, when they have the means and opportunity, and endure the rest. A gentleman connected with shipbuilding, and also on the Board of the Poor-house of the district, informed the writer that when the shipbuilding became dull and the men had to be discharged, it was the wives of the skilled workmen, to whom he had been paying wages for months of £2, £3, and £3 10s. a week, who were the first to ask relief. Not for about a month afterwards came the wives of the labourers who attended upon them, and whose wages were from eighteen to twenty shillings. Low wage or high wage is a matter that should only concern the people directly interested. The lowest is well above the amount required for household expenses, if the workman likes ; the highest is not enough, if he does not like. It is the abuse and the stoppage of the wage, whatever its amount, that brings poverty.

As slavery gave place to free labour, the wages of the free labourer were calculated on the work of the slave—the value of his weekly production or output,

less the price of his living.   There was no other way.
Slavery was not all abolished at once ; is not yet ; and
the freeman had to compete with forced labour.   If
he were not profitable to his employer there was no
need for him.

It is claimed by business and professional men that
they are workers equally with the physical labourer,
some asserting that brain work is harder than manual
labour.   The claim cannot be admitted as regards
equality of conditions.   There is not a brain worker
who would exchange his occupation for one of toil :
there is not a labourer who would not exchange his
occupation for one of business ; there is not a neutral
person without experience of either, when compelled to
choose, would choose the pickaxe in preference to the
pen.   The manual labourer stands alone in his pecu-
liarity.   He cannot multiply himself like the merchant
or manufacturer.   He cannot extend his labour beyond
himself.   He cannot accumulate his labour to live upon
it in his old age.   He cannot depute it to younger
men when he grows old, and yet reap the profits of it.
He cannot sell it when he wants to retire.   Throughout
life he can never increase his capital, but must always
draw upon it.   His greatest period of productivity
(and therefore high wages, where permissible) is when
he has least responsibilities (early manhood), and so he
learns improvidence and the love of spending money
(having no one but himself to keep) ; and as he advances
in life his energy fails and his burdens increase.   Now
let us look at even the small tradesman.   By a single
thought he may see how he may save upon a transaction ; but the thought is as applicable to five hundred
transactions of the same kind, and he can reap the
profit from all these as easily as one.   Thus this
tradesman multiplies himself by five hundred in one
action.   If he finds out how to save in the making up

of his goods, it does not apply to one occasion only
but may be repeated as often as he makes a sale. But
when the workman makes a stroke with the hammer
or a heave with the spade, these actions cannot repeat
themselves without renewed labour. If the manufacturer can make a profit out of the employment of one
man, the more men he employs the greater the profit,
and the one transaction may cost him no more thought,
and therefore " work," than the other. The small
tradesman can open a branch in a neighbouring sub-
urb, and superintend both. He is thus as it were two
tradesmen ; he also can conduct a business at a
distance in another town through servants ; but the
poor workman cannot. The workman can toilfully
save his wages against his old age, but a tradesman
does not need. A well-conducted business accumulates
and increases of itself and after twenty or thirty years
its owner can live upon it when he can do it no good.
Thrift not being a natural gift in man, generally only
those can practise it who have a strong interest in the
process, and an ever-present feeling of reward for their
self denial, to encourage them and help them to contend with every new desire that arises from the
knowledge that they have the means to indulge it.
The smallest independent worker, small tradesman, or
shopkeeper, even the pedlar, has ever before him this
inducement to encourage him to thrift. Every additional penny he can add to his business he knows makes
his labours less and his profits greater. " Capital !
more capital !" is his cry, and all that he can save is
added to his stock. The workman has no such encouragement to save his money. His life is rounded
off in so many pay days. When he has received
his wages the world is quits with him, and a new
week is a new contract. There is no continuity in
his interests that binds him to the world, as there is in

business life, by which he is called upon to make any sacrifice.

So far we have sought to show the natural disadvantages of the man who labours for hire, instead of, as Nature meant him, for himself. To this must be added another one for which we are partly indebted to the appliance of machinery to all kinds of industry, and partly to the men themselves. Before the introduction of machinery, there were no large individual employers of labour, but there were many small ones. There were no railways, no steamships, nothing that required large works, or ponderous machinery. Coal was only needed for domestic consumption. All therefore that was made or manufactured was done so in a very small way, and to embark in trade for one's self required little or no capital. Everybody with the slightest ambition could begin business for himself. Few masters employed more than two or three men, and each man therefore learned his whole business thoroughly. The people who therefore sought employment were of two classes : the lazy and unambitious, and the active and ambitious. It was only the former who meant to be a workman all his life. The latter looked upon wage-earning as a necessary but intermediate condition. Through it he could best learn his trade, and wait for the proper opportunity to begin on his own behalf. Diverse as these motives were they were both willing to serve for a wage that left a considerable margin of profit to the employer ; or in other words, a living wage and no more—the unambitious one, because if he could live upon it, that was all his concern ; and the ambitious one, because the spirit of the master was already in him and to increase wages as a servant was to cut his throat when a master. The revolution then which machinery wrought was this ; the workmen only learned a section of the

process of manufacture, or an insignificant part of his
trade. This was a fatal blow to his ever becoming a
master on his own account. He again became a slave,
this time not to his employer, but to his machine.
Without it he was useless. Machinery required
capital, and the number of workmen who could start
for themselves under the new conditions was further
reduced. But the forcing up of wages by strikes and
other artificial means, so reduced the margin of profit
on each man's hire, that the only recourse for the
employer was to recoup himself by increasing the
number employed. Works were increased, extra
capital invested, newer and more improved machinery
erected, until it required a fortune, or a limited liability
company to conduct a single work. The last hope of
any workman being able to begin for himself in any of
the great staple industries of the country has vanished,
and he may reflect that he has helped to throw himself
back into the slavery from which he sprung : this time
he is a slave to his trade.

At the present day thousands of men are born to a
trade, or part of a trade, in which they know their whole
lives are to be spent as wage-earners. They know the end
from the beginning. Their aspirations, ambitions, and
desires are confined within its limits, and within these
limits what can they fasten upon, what interest themselves in ? An increase of wage. For what purpose ?
To save ? to accumulate for the purpose of beginning
business ? to invest ? to improve their condition of
life ? None of these ; merely, while it lasts to have a
pleasant roughness of money with them. That is the
average working man's highest ideal. For that, they
employ agitators and organizers : for that, they endure
strikes : for that, they go idle when there is plenty of
work. How are the interests of the employer and
employed to be conjoined ? When will the wages

question ever be settled? The masters are bound
hand and foot by Economic law, they cannot employ
labour unless it is remunerative. The agitator refuses
to recognise any Economic law in the employment of
labour.

Of the philanthropist, and all who have the happiness
of the wage-earner at heart, we ask that they read
these lines carefully. They will see plainly that of all
people in the world, the conditions of the toiler's life
should not be interfered with. It is unique in its
limitations, and there are none but the employer and
his workmen know the variations of these limits.
Perhaps in the whole working life of a labourer they
may never have averaged more than ten per cent. for and
against. Every strike costs the workman more than he
gains whether he win his purpose or not, and the most
laudable thing the well-wisher of the workmen can do,
is to stand aside and be silent, when men are on
strike. It is only fair to both parties, and it will
reduce the strike in regard to time to small compass,
thereby saving the men furthur expenditure. Strikes
will come; but they will be of short duration, and little
harm done if the two parties are left alone. If you
think to interfere where you can only do harm, advise
the workman to take a lower wage. He will not do so;
but if all those who take upon themselves to advise the
workman were giving him this advice, it would have
the effect of keeping him longer at a stable wage than
at present. It is essential to the happiness of the
workman that he should have stability of conditions, a
long spell at the same rate of wages, so that his habits
should get solidified, and he learns to put his money to
its best use. At high-pressure wages there are a
great many in every trade who never get a constant
twelvemonths' employment. If the workmen would
take a shade less wages, the employer could give all,

constant employment, and so the men would earn more
in the year though less per week.

On the other hand, see the harm to the workmen and
the trade of the country the agitator can do when he
can get the support of the public outside. The
memorable dockers' strike in London was the first of
any magnitude in which the public were cozened to
take a part. Immediately the public became interested
the real point in dispute was pushed to the back-
ground. The agitator at every street corner, and the press
in every issue, poured forth most eloquently upon the
hard life of the docker generally, his small wage, his
struggles every morning for employment, and his mode
of living. All of which is as pertinent to him one day as
another, one year as another, whether he is on strike or
full employment at top wages. But it prejudiced the
public, and was a great injustice to the Dock company.
Their numbers may be small but they are entitled to
even-handed justice. The moneys of widows and
orphans may have been in their keeping ; why are they
not also to be considered ? Lord Macaulay says that
the people of England have a fit of madness every ten
years, over something or another, and London appears
to have one specially on its own account in the interval.
It lost its head over the dockers, as it had over
slumming. Cheques poured in upon the organizers ;
the coffers were kept full, being renewed every day by
sympathisers, and the docker had a much better time in
idleness than when at work.

This tangible form of sympathy cost the workmen
of this country in a few years over a million sterling of
wages, in addition to making their future employment
more difficult by the disorganisation of business ; but
above all it introduced a new element into the question
of wages and strikes that will cost them twenty
million more if they pursue it. The organisers and

agents of the men agreed that strikes in future must be carefully dressed up to win the approval of the public, their sympathy, and cash. To do so the most effective way was to make as many of them (the public) suffer as possible, and those living too remote from the scene of action have their minds filled with the magnitude of numbers. This was the way the succeeding strikes were engineered—the midland colliers' strike, the seamen's strike at Hull, the Scotch railway strike, and colliery strike. It was most pitiful to see those agitators, for weeks before the strike, showing their anxiety and eagerness to work up the public sympathy. Public utterances everywhere, platform speeches every night, and press communications daily, all addressed to the public. Deputations carefully chosen to entrap the masters in an unenviable light. Great cry for arbitration, while putting every obstacle in its way. And so the poor workmen were held like dogs in a leash ; if the public would rise to the sport, then they would get value for their money ; but if not, the strike either never took place, or it fizzled out like a damp squib.

The public sympathy cannot for long be maintained on sordid questions of whether it is sixpence per day up, or sixpence per day down. They must have some soul-satisfying principle to pour their sentiments over, and the agitator is quite willing to supply them. A principle may be anything, and can be sprung upon the employer at any time irrespective of the contentment of the men, the state of trade, or the briskness or dulness of any particular occupation. It may be the eight-hours question ; it may be whom they choose to allow the employer to take on, or pay off ; it can at all times be the everlasting principle that wages are too low for the agitator's liking. Here is an instance, and we must state our authority is the public press in their daily report of the proceedings : Mr. Tom Mann, in his

report of the Dockers' Union of London, said that the
hindrance to his endeavours to gain an increase in
wages for them was their own suicidal or cutthroat
competition. Here was the confession of a leader
meditating a strike without the workmen's consent, or
with that kind of consent that said he was welcome to
do so if he could do it without them. They were too
much engaged in attending to their own affairs. There
were more labourers than work, and they who had it
were anxious to keep it, and those who were idle were
trying to get a share of the employment, even at a
lower rate of wages, which we take to be the cutthroat
or suicidal competition Mr. Mann complained of. The
dockers had no grievance to mend, no quarrel with their
employers to adjust, no discontent with their labour, no
sense of injustice to brood over, yet their paid servant
or organiser was meditating to destroy this harmonious
state of things and provoke a strike ! There was no
ground as between employer and employed to fix a
quarrel or strike upon. How then was it to be done ?
We do not know, but we presume on the general
principle that wages are always too low. We have
heard language from this gentleman and some of his
friends, from which the only deduction one can reasonably make is that in their opinion the wages of the
workmen are too low, and continue to be too low, and
no matter what happens will ever remain too low. Here
then is a declared enemy to any settlement of the
industrial question. In this case he was only defeated
by the individuality of the men themselves. To them,
to keep in employment personally was more desirable
than helping Mr. Mann to successfully assert his principle.
But will it always be so ? The very slightest friction
between master and men might have raised a feeling in
the men that would have made them give ear to the
agitator and his principle.

It would make one despair of ever seeing a happy and contented working class, to think that every trade of any dimensions pays one or more persons whose business is to watch and take advantage of every change in the condition of trade, no matter how insignificant, to assert claims they know cannot be admitted, and attempt to enforce them through the suffering of the men themselves. But above all things, whether there is any change in the conditions of labour or no, they must never allow the question to be settled. The relations of the men and masters must never be allowed to reach that point from which harmony and goodwill might engender. The sea must never be calm, the day must know no rest, the armies must not fraternize. Unrest, turmoil, and suspicion are now the relationship between master and man ; and to keep them properly apart the agitator makes himself the intermediary through whom all communications must pass. In one sense, the employer hires his man from the agitator. It is he who allows them to work ; he who fixes the conditions of their hire ; he to whom all disputes must be referred ; and he who takes them away when he likes. But the devil has a halt ; and the schemes of men are imperfect because they are unnatural, and Nature is the only perfect thing in this world. There is one thing that will always militate against the triumph of the agitator's principles. Since the public have sympathized with the workmen on strike, the workman now expects to be paid for striking. It then lies with the public to put an end to strikes by taking no part in them whatever. They are not in a position to judge in the matter, and to take one side is to wrong the other, as no matter which side they support they are encouraging that side to continue the strike longer than they otherwise would ; and every hour and every day a person helps to continue a strike he is doing the worst service to his friends he possibly could. Without outside support no strike would last more than a week or so, and, best of all, they would never rise to the importance of attracting public attention ; and when they fail in that, the agitator's occupation is gone, and industrial peace may visit the land.

We have referred before to the workman's demand that the State or municipalities should protect him from ever being out of employment.

The demand is unique in its selfishness. The great army of warehousemen and clerks are exactly in the same position as the artisan. They are liable to dismissal any minute, and they are subject to all the vicissitudes of dull trade, contraction of employment, &c., that the workman is. And worse, they work as long, and in many cases longer hours, for less pay. But, of course, they have no agitators to imagine their wrongs for them. When severe industrial depression overtakes this country, the suicides never belong to the workman class ; they generally come from the poor clerk brigade. For them there is no philanthropical schemes, no demands for permanent employment, no parliamentary consideration of their condition. They are allowed to endure their distress alone, until endurance itself seeks relief in the river.

We have been surprised lately to see that this preposterous demand (natural enough in the mouths of the agitator and the invertebrate parliamentarian) should be accepted as a matter-of-course by magazine writers, philosophers, and students of the industrial question—people who are supposed to think and write on the question impartially. Without justification or argument they have adopted the doctrine as if it were a settled principle of the conditions of labour. "Of course," says the latest of these writers, "the workman *must* be found employment."

The desire for municipal workshops so strongly advo-
cated by the workmen's leaders as a solution of the
unemployed question, is twofold ; and the reason given
to the public is not the paramount one.   If a town
started a workshop it would have to give the highest
conditions in all respects, the most extreme demands
to its employés, pay the highest wages, grant the
shortest hours, &c., without any consideration of
economy.   Then the agitator would use this artificial
condition of labour, as a lever to raise all private
employment to the same level.   But let us see if
municipal workshops would even perform the services
required of them.   The Government have just now some
royal dockyards, in which they repair, overhaul, and build
our navy, and have also added making their engines.
There are also throughout the country plenty of shipyards
and engine works.   When these latter are empty, how
many men thrown out of employment do, or can, these
State works find work for?   Precious few, if any.
They have their own staff of workmen, and they have
no room for more.   Just so would it be with the
municipal works.   They would be bound to have
a permanent staff.   The conditions of labour in them
being more favourable than with private employers,
they would be "rushed" by the men to get into them.
Once they were full, the men would not leave, and the
managers could not discharge them.   The town dare
never close the works and set them all adrift again.   No
matter how brisk trade became, they would hold there
would always be plenty of men to overtake it.   Then
when a period of dulness came again, what room would
our municipal workshops have for absorbing the unemployed?   None, none whatever ; while the work would
be carried on at a fearful loss.

The Admiralty, however, have another way of finding
work for the unemployed, a most excellent way, and one

we would strongly recommend to the philanthropist and the municipalities. When private shipyards and engineering shops are idle, the Admiralty give out to these works as many orders as it can, and keep the men in employment until better times come. Now let us see how that would do if adopted by the towns to give their citizens employment.

Nearly every large town is identified with and dependent upon one special industry. In some it is cotton, some lace, some ironwork, some chemicals, and it can only be when that particular industry was dull, that there could be any real distress. What then is to hinder the town giving the employers sufficient work to keep their men engaged until orders come, in the usual way again? With anything like care it could be done at very little expense, sometimes at a profit. When an industry is dull, its raw material is generally very cheap ; the employer is willing to take very little for making, would often be glad to get cost price, rather than shut his works and waste his machinery, and the wages of the workmen would also have to be reduced. As the whole thing is done for his, the workman's, benefit, he must also share some part of the sacrifice. And in spite of his leaders he would, because public opinion would be against him. With such all-round reductions the manufactured article would come out at a low cost, and might either be sold in the market at once, or stored against a rise. Private manufacturers make money this way ; why should the town not do it without much loss ? All the town has to do, if it were textile fabrics that was the principal business, was to settle the price with the manufacturers, and the quantity (not allowing them to do more than enough to keep their regular hands going), and either let them sell the material or store it, whichever seemed most profitable, the town indemnifying the manufacturer against any loss.

Almost all kinds of manufactures could be dealt with
in this way, subject to some alterations of details
necessary from the nature of the material and the
rules of its trade.   Even ships could be built upon this
plan.   There are many private owners of shipyards
who lay down the keels of boats for themselves when
their slips are bare.   They have their staff to keep
any way, and their machinery is best working, while
they have a natural desire to keep their workmen
together as long as they can.   Sometimes the workmen
are told what is intended, and are asked to take a less
rate of wages.   These boats are often sold before they
are launched, and if not at a great profit, seldom at a
loss.   All that a shipbuilding town has to do, is to
settle the price per ton of a handy steamer of a
popular size and tonnage, and let the shipbuilder sell
it if he can, or submit offers.   If the town got cost
price, it should take it.   Its purpose is not to make a
profit, but to keep its shipworking population employed
without loss.

Let us look at the advantages of this system over
the known disadvantages of the other.   The cost
would be less, and, managed with an honest intention,
might be infinitesimal even, compared with the useless
alternative of stone-breaking, where one parish would
sell for £5 what cost it between £70 and £80.   It
would free the city from requiring to invest any capital
in works, and as regards expenditure the town would
always be free to stop or reduce its contracts as· it saw
fit.   The workmen would continue at the employment
to which they were trained, and engaged in which they
were most profitably exercised.   They would not even
have to change employers, and so could remain in
their houses, &c., as usual.   The conditions of labour
would not be disturbed in any way ; and the continuous
circulation of wages would also keep in their wonted

prosperity all the tradesmen that depend upon the
wage-earner : the butcher, baker, grocer, clothier, &c.
In fact, the prosperity of the town would be continuous
and unremitting.   Only the true and honest workman
would be benefited by this process, and that alone
would show the immense army of loafers who are
ever ready to join the unemployed and share their
charity.   All this would be saved.   And last of all, it
is a plan by which even-handed justice is served all
round.   The proprietors who are always ignored, are
here considered with the rest.   They make no pecuniary
gain, but their works are kept going, their men continue with them, their business goes on as usual, and
when business becomes brisk again, they are ready for
it without trouble and expense.   All the tradesmen
who deal with the working classes, and are bound
more or less to give them credit, would also be considered.   While the workmen got their wages regularly, the tradesmen they dealt with would get their
accounts, and continued business.   At present, when
men are out of employment, of course they have no
money to pay their tradesmen, and soon no clothing or
furniture.   Then, when charity sets in, it comes from a
rich quarter of the town that buys the food from its
own tradesmen.   All debts by the Poor are repudiated.
They are fed ; and their poor tradesmen are starved.
Then when the game is over, the workman seeks for
work in another quarter, and is heard of no more.

CHAPTER VIII

THE SUBMERGED TENTH

The submerged tenth—Instances of the preference for voluntary
poverty over social repression—Their lives and habits—
Examination of the plans for their redemption—Their great
industrial value—Philanthropy useless ; a lower civilisation
or simpler form of life needed.

THE condition of industrial and social life at the
present day is one of severe repression, and the idea
possessed by so many of our teachers that the only
virtue is Uniformity, is steadily acting to make that
repression more and more severe. Every action that
is not a free and spontaneous one is the product of
repression ; and when we consider that the inhibitive
or repressive faculty is the weakest mental quality we
possess, we may guess the amount of mental friction
continually going on within us from this constant
subordination of natural impulse to socially approved
action. It is this brain-wear that makes lunatics,
hystericals, and a great many of the Poor. From
childhood to old age we are drilled, dragooned, mar-
shalled, and ordered about until many are incapable
of any action of their own initiative. They require
the support of the knowledge that some person has
done it before. But on the other hand, the burden

of life becomes too great for many to bear, and they
fall from the ranks, no longer able to march with their
neighbours. And when they fall they fall, like Lucifer,
never wishing to rise again. When they reach bottom,
there they find a large proportion of their fellow-men
who have voluntarily proposed to themselves to remain
poor because of its many advantages. There are two
forms of life open to every citizen, the high and the
low. They are both perfectly legal ; but because the
moralist has chosen the high one, he condemns the low
one as immoral. The high life is the utmost expenditure of energy, to make the most money, to purchase
the largest amount of pleasure ; the low is the reverse
—the least expenditure of energy, no more than enough
to meet temporary needs, and to extract pleasure from
life wherever and whenever it presents itself. The
toiler thinks there is little pleasure in life, because he
is always working, and when he has leisure he has not
the money to purchase pleasure ; but these citizens
we refer to know better, infinitely better, than the
philanthropist, who talks of their lives being dull,
and grey, and monotonous, and requiring brighten-
ing up : they know that to a person of leisure who
studies the question thoroughly a large city affords a
continual succession of free amusements. After a
trial of both forms of life, the submerged tenth have
chosen the lower for its advantages. In the high life,
which all are condemned to try first, they found they
had to work like a machine from a certain hour to a
certain hour, day after day. Their leisure had to be
spent in conformity with the opinion of their neighbours. They had to dress to please their neighbour.
They had to hold the same opinions. Their neighbour
chose their amusements for them. Even the disposal
of their money was not free from judgment and
opinion. They had to buy things they did not want

because their neighbour bought them, and give away
money because he gave. There was no room for
natural action in their lives, no freedom, no liberty.
And the only reward to them for all this slavery and
repression was their neighbour's good opinion, which
was not sincere.

In the low life they found all the conditions they
appreciated — freedom, irresponsibility, relief from
monotony, the pleasure of following every whim, ex-
emption from the worry of respectability, and unlimited leisure. This is the life the Rich aim at and
cannot attain ; this class can attain it without wealth.
All they have to pay for the pleasure of this form of
existence is a little bodily discomfort occasionally, not
enough for any man of ordinary courage and endurance to cry out about—an empty stomach for a day,
too light clothing for a sudden frost, and an occasional
bed without pillow or blankets. But custom develops
a high form of endurance, and experience soon reduces
the chances of these things happening to a minimum,
until their possibility is no longer a consideration.

Drawn from all classes of society, this community
has three characteristics, any one of which is a sufficient cause for this life being agreeable to its owner.
There are the people of low natural energy, who never
could compete with their fellow-men in a day's work.
These people have retired from the battle of life in
disgust. Impossible to fulfil their natural desires by
their labour, they reverse the process, and suppress
desire to a point considerably below their powers of
achievement. It is the more easy to do this, as their
desires generally flow as weakly as their energy. Then
there are the unambitious people, strong enough and
healthy enough, but who do not see in the aims and
aspirations of their fellow-men anything very desirable,
and certainly no reasonable compensation for the labour

necessary to attain them. To such a class a low form
of life is natural. They work at odd times, but leisure
becomes dearer to them as it is enjoyed, and latterly
only their necessities drive them to legitimate employment. But the great majority are people of a different
stamp. Mostly descended at one time or another from
the better classes, they have some education, sometimes their mental strength exceeding their physical.
Their principal characteristic is a mercurial tempera-
ment and an incapacity to follow any system of order
or uniformity. Regularity is unendurable ; they must
follow the whim of the moment. Their desires are
evanescent, but for the time being impressive, and one
gives way to another so rapidly, that ere they can act
to fulfil one, another has superseded it, as brilliant, as
commanding, and as exigeant. They thus become accustomed to let their desires exhaust themselves without any attempt at fulfilment—the simplest plan where
possible, and in their case the only one, as they have no
power of restraint. These people could not work as
civilisation demands that men should work. The consciousness that their hours and actions were under
some other authority than themselves would soon
make the position too irksome, and the reward, no
matter how great, falls in value as the irritation increases. Nor is this only in physical wage-earning
labour. Some of them have been in affluent positions,
with nothing to do but sit in their office from ten to
four, but the restraint was unendurable. Punctuality
and duty are impossibilities ; they are equally monotonous, and would require a brain-service that would
be too exhausting.

These people are the true philosophers of life ;
they are its natural humourists. All the ambitions
and desires they daily see others strive for, groan over,
and, ultimately failing in, give way to despair, are to

them quite unworthy, and therefore amusing. They see people striving and quarrelling, deceiving and cheating for objects as indifferent to them as the fate of the butterfly they sometimes chase. Their inability to appreciate the aims of others gives them a healthy contempt for their mental calibre ; and their disbelief in anything as a motor of action but a keen and pressing self-interest (the only thing that moves them to action) gives them a rooted scepticism in disinterestedness. Their low estimation of the ordinary aspirations of their fellowman makes them feel that nothing but a powerful incentive to something great and noble could stir *them* to action, and they are grateful that that incentive never comes.

Being indifferent to other men's motives, they are also indifferent to the laws that govern other men in their relations and actions one to another. They play upon the sympathies of the charitable without compunction : they hoax the missions, and lay in wait for the philanthropist. They are equally ready to demonstrate as the unemployed—the nearest the truth of all their demonstrations—or for local veto—the furthest from the truth of all their demonstrations. Like stage supernumeraries, they are ready to be a bridal chorus or a destroying army. Having no convictions themselves they are ready to play upon the convictions of others. Having no enthusiasm they admire it in others, and omit no opportunity of stimulating it, because enthusiasm is inclined to be generous. Having leisure they cultivate their minds : they know all the favourite topics of the day, and are ever willing to enlighten their duller but wealthier brethren in exchange for drinks and other small perquisites. They know the nature and rules and modes of application of all the charities and missions. They are familiar with every form of free entertainment from the Sunday

breakfast to the Christmas dinner. They are posted
as to every public and private entertainment where
largesse and gifts form a part. They are ever on the
watch for a sympathetic listener, and a politician might
envy them the genius—from practice—with which they
can strike the topic that will soonest lead to the
main chance.

When the pinch arises they can sing a hymn with
fervour in exchange for a breakfast, and then burlesque
the performance to a person for a drink to wash it
down. With seeming repentance they will outsit a
sermon upon their sins for a pair of trousers, then
entertain a few friends with a highly-caricatured version
of the service, and the proceeds of the trousers. The
fault does not lie with them, but with those who sell
breakfasts for hymn-singing, and trousers for sermon-
hearing. These characters are no more sincere in their
burlesques than in their piety; they are selling their
talents for what they will fetch. They are all things to
all men, that will make life easy for them.

This section is of course the leaders of the others;
the others admire their genius and talent, and follow
them like lambs. These people are in reality the Poor.
They are the people whom the philanthropist and the
missioner meet; they are the deputationers; they are
the only articulate section of the Poor; they are the
unemployed in all his stages. They are also the workman; it is they, and not he, who are always demanding
his rights, and are eloquent upon his grievances. It is
their desire to make labour as remunerative as possible;
they are still compelled to work a little, and work to
them is more hateful than to any other of God's
creatures. It is not therefore for the big wage, but
because less work would do. The Economic laws of
labour are their special detestation; they savour of order
and regularity and proportion; to suspend them is

their great desire so that they could work when they chose, and fix their own remuneration.

These are the people upon whom the social reformer in all his phases has spent his years of energy, and his endless subscriptions. He has been helping to make life easy for them, and more firmly rooting them in their chosen life. He has had truly a disheartening task. Their desires are so small he could interest them in nothing ; their interests so slight he could root them to nothing. They have no possessions to assail, no affections to threaten, no faith to undermine. They have no yesterday to remember or regret ; no to-morrow to hope for, or to fear. They know only the day when it comes, and the best and easiest mode of enjoying it.

These are the people for whom so much more is intended. Over-sea colonies, and at home Industrial farms. Of the over-sea colonies it is premature to speak. We only hear occasionally of their progress in regard to the settlement of locality, &c., and it seems that it will require the income of a real colony to work one of them. Of the industrial farms we have more precise data. How is anything in the country going to attract these people from the cities, where all their pleasures are, and their opportunities? The country cannot compete with the towns just now to any man where the wages are equal, because of the greater attractions and pleasures of the latter. How is it possible to attract to the country people who only live for pleasure, and who only know the pleasures of a large city? Why do all the wealthy people of the country flock to London ? Yet the same people wonder why the Poor gravitate to the cities. There are some politicians anxious to put the people back upon the land. They will find that a more difficult task than they imagine. It will not be the getting of the land, or of money to

stock it, or work it, but the getting the people themselves to surrender the pleasures of city life for the
country. Again, how is it possible to induce people
who hate work and love freedom, to go into these
glorified poor-houses and completely change their
nature, and take kindly to regular employment and
continued supervision? If these people wanted work,
they could get it in the city on more remunerative
terms than that of semi-pauperisation ; if they had been
desirous of leading a regular life they could have done
so under more favourable conditions than that of compulsion. Everybody who knows them, and has come
in contact with them, has been using every endeavour
he thought would be effectual in encouraging and
seeking to help these people to lead regular lives—their
friends, the missionaries, their workman neighbours,
and even the police.

But the question is not, Who will patronise these
institutions? Somebody no doubt will, as there are
always curious and impulsive people who rejoice in
experiments. Were these institutions thirty times as
numerous as they are so far projected, they could be all
filled to overflowing, and the submerged tenth live and
enjoy itself in the cities as usual. Supposing these
institutions absorbed the whole of the floating Poor of
the present day ; what then? In another year or so
there would be another submerged tenth to deal with.
These people are the product of civilisation, and
civilisation is continuing to make them at an ever-
increasing pace. What matters carrying away the
overflow of a fountain in buckets if the fountain is
allowed to flow on ? But the mission-maker is so proud
of his idea that he shuts his ears and his eyes to every
evidence that his mission is not fulfilling the purpose
for which it was designed. Only keep him busy and
that is enough for him ; it is his one and only great

argument of success. If there are people found to go
to the over-sea colony, then it will be a great success,
whether these people could pay their own passage or
not, whether they are tramps wanting to do the
colonies, sailors shifting to a new port without wanting
to work their passage, tradesmen who want to do the
tramp, or that large class of exuberant youth who want
to go abroad, and are governed in their choice by the
cheapness of the journey—all these may keep the over-
sea scheme busy, not one of those for whom it is meant.
But the public will only hear in glowing praise the
numbers patronising it, and the urgent necessity for
funds. In like manner the industrial farm will be the
country representative of the casual ward, and all the
tramps in passing may have a turn at it. There are in
the city and country hundreds to whom it may be
useful, the workman passing from one centre of industry
to another, the deserter and the town loafer when
things become too hot for him, and workmen on strike.
All these can make a country casual ward useful at times,
but none but the philanthropist imagines that because
these people take advantage of the farm when they
want to, that they bind themselves to any alteration of
their mode of life afterwards. If the farms fill as they
must fill—because once started they will go on raising
the inducements until they attract guests—then the fact
that they are filled will be the philanthropist's all-
satisfying evidence of success, although they have been
forced to raise the attractions so high that they are
enticing people from honest labour.

That the philanthropist looks no further himself for
evidence of the success of his mission, but also has
persuaded the public to accept as sole criterion the fact
of his being well patronised, we give a particular
instance. When the great frost of the beginning of the
present year came on, the city of Glasgow began relief-

works. In its usual way it began with small inducements and many precautions, and ended in reckless,
almost criminal, liberality and extravagance. At the
beginning the usual " deserving cases only " farce was
attempted, and something under a hundred applicants
per day appeared. But as there is no city keeps an
organisation able to compete with periods of sudden
and temporary distress, the personal inquiry business
broke down. Then two and three hundred appeared
not afraid of the superficial questions that were put to
them. The Lord Provost invited subscriptions to meet
the expenses, and money rolled in upon him harder
than it could be used, breadstuffs were sent daily by
the tons, and unlimited parcels of clothing from
manufacturers, merchants, and warehousemen. Then
the saturnalia began ; anybody and everybody could get
warm meals, food, orders upon tradesmen to the value
of three or four shillings' worth, clothing of all descrip-
tions, and in some cases money. People left their work
to have a share in the plunder while it lasted, and by
the computation of one of the newspapers the number
of applicants for relief rose in one week from seven
hundred to twenty thousand. With an unanimity that
was wonderful *all the press* accepted this great increase
of numbers as a sad evidence of how widespread the
distress had become. None seemed to think the reason
lay in the town having recklessly made the conditions
of charity more profitable than honest employment.

But to return to the submerged tenth. These
people we have said are the product of civilisation,
rather we should say the by-product of over-civilisation.
They principally belong to the English-speaking people,
and the English-speaking people pride themselves they
are in the van of civilisation. They are the tramp of
America, the sundowner of Australia, and the loafer at
home. The laws of their country they may endure ; the

vagaries of municipal legislation is a severe trial ; but
beyond these, to be hounded, bullied, and worried by
the demands of the social reformer, the pietist, and
moralist, let alone the teetotaller, is only to be borne
by the strong and the dull—the one who goes on his
way unheeding, and the other who goes on his way un-
knowing.   Civilisation may go on year after year
adding to the demands it makes upon the citizen, but if
it does not make citizens with strength enough to bear
these demands then the process of accumulating
submerged tenths must continue.

With the exception of the Autolycus-like habit of
keeping a very keen eye on the unconsidered trifles of
others—for what are unconsidered trifles to others are
often a day's commissariat to them—these people are
innocent of offence.   But they are at deadly enmity
with the social reformer, who to them is the incarnation
of all evil.   His baleful eye is ever upon them ; he is always
reminding the police of their duty toward them ; he is
ever at the ear of the city council asking for further
powers to crush them ; he sighs and groans in the
churches over them, and resurrects old and musty
statutes to annoy and harass them. His soul is
steeped in the dull uniformity of his own habits.   He
cannot sleep at night to think of these people going
to bed when they like, or not at all.   He cannot work
with any pleasure when he thinks that these people, so
much beneath him, only work when they choose.

Yet a town can better allow them to remain as harmless as they are than drive them to worse, and any
attempt to force them into habits that they hate will
only tend to make them swell the criminal classes.
The question is not a moral one.   They are not
criminal for the same reason that they are not
workmen, they do not want its labour, they do not
want its reward, and it imperils their freedom ; but if

their present life is made too difficult, then they will
have to make a choice.

Now let us look at the other side—the industrial
value of the submerged tenth.   It is a worthy comment
upon the bias and prejudice of the philanthropist and
social reformer, that in the submerged tenth they have
never looked for another side, or suspected an industrial value.   Professing to study the lives of the
Poor, they have gone among them only looking for
what they expected and wanted to find, their objectionable habits, thriftlessness, drunkenness, and irregular
lives.

The submerged tenth fills a most important place in
the industrial economy of all large towns.   They are the
reserve forces of trade ; its governors or regulators.
They protect its sudden demands and expansions from
bringing on crises and disorganisation, and they allow its
contractions to act gently and evenly without creating
disorder and distress.   In the normal condition of trade
all the regular workmen are employed ; no trade keeps
a staff of unemployed.   Where, then, would the extra
supply come from in periods of inflation ?   In every
trade there are times of temporary necessity where,
for a day or so, a large staff is required.   Where are
these to be found ?   No employer can keep a staff for
emergencies.   When all regular men are employed,
there is the necessity for an army of odd-job men.   No
corporation could keep a squad of men for temporary
purposes.   There is no class could fill these requirements but the submerged tenth.   All regular workmen
base their lives upon regular pay ; cessation of work
means poverty, and if trade is dull in their town they
leave it, or try to get employment in some other trade.
Only people to whom idleness is the natural condition
of life could make temporary employment profitable.
Idleness to them is no hardship, and temporary employ-

ment is attractive and enjoyable. Almost all the loafers
have a trade and have to work occasionally, but when
wages are high, managers become pressed for men and
therefore indulgent, and discipline is relaxed, then the
loafer under the freer conditions can work a little longer,
perhaps long enough till the crisis is past. Then when
he is discharged the conditions of trade are not affected,
he goes back to his natural element of idleness. Thus
the loafer fills a place of the utmost importance to
industry, a place no other class could take. Upon him
the elasticity of trade depends. The workman is indebted to him for his own constant employment. The
employer is indebted to him for meeting his temporary
demands without extra cost. The philanthropist is
indebted to him that poverty is neither more abundant
nor more acute, as he acts as a buffer between the
regular workman and bad times. And the whole community is indebted to him because he gives both a
pliability and stability to the general conditions of trade,
being the only section of the community that can be
absorbed in its expansions and thrown off in its contractions without harm or inconvenience.

No philanthropy can touch this people ; no society
for improving the condition of the Poor affect them.
All such efforts will only confirm them in the mode of
life they find best adapted to their natures. Only an
alteration in the laws that have made them what they
are could arrest their further growth. What they want
is a lower civilisation, greater individual freedom, less
demands upon them for the benefit of others. The old
reformers fought for freedom ; the social reformers aim
at social slavery. The English idea of civilisation is
the endless manufacture of legislation ; laws that follow
you into your house ; laws that follow you into your
business ; that pursue you upon the street, and mix with
your pleasures. The citizen lying buried beneath tons

of personal legislation is its apotheosis. What effect has it upon the stranger, to be shown the orderliness of our citizen's lives, when afterwards he finds that orderliness was not their own, was not voluntary, but that they were slaves to a hundred statutes that governed every act of their lives? A trained monkey was as good a type of civilisation. From such restraint neither strength nor virtue can grow. The over-legislated has no room for the exercise of his natural inclination to virtue. All incentive is stamped out of him. If the law will have its very large pound of flesh, there is no inclination to add to it voluntary contributions.

The highest form of civilisation should be based upon the greatest freedom of the citizen and the lowest limit of enactment. A few broad comprehensive statutes should be all that are required. The evidence of the civilisation should lie in, and be seen in, the conduct of the citizen, and to cultivate the highest virtues a man must have the greatest freedom.

Supposing there was no new law permitted to be passed in this country for a hundred years. Instead of flying to Parliament for legislation for every petty grievance and dispute, men would have to turn to some other mode of settling their differences. Among the modes available, compromise would be the most popular. This would be the first bringing together of your own and your neighbour's interests, although it is after the action. The next step would be to make the compromise easy; both you and your neighbour would seek to keep any difference that might arise between you as narrow as possible, never allowing it to grow to proportions that could be either serious or annoying. From that step to the next is natural and unavoidable, namely, to consider your neighbour's interests with your own before the action, to avoid the possibility of friction. The only way the human mind has of performing this operation is by leaning palpably to "virtue's side," or, in other words, making your actions as profitable to your neighbour as your own interests will permit. Here lies the root-matter of all virtue. It is free from all self-sacrifice, which is unnatural; but it includes all the mutual consideration, mutual help, and mutual support the world requires. There would be no quarrels, no anger, no disputes; no necessity for law unless the few broad principles already specified, required more as a guide to action than as a restraint; no interference with personal liberty in any form; while the citizen, and not the Statute Book, would be the nation's exponent of civilisation.

CHAPTER IX

SOME MISSIONS.—THE ATTITUDE OF THE POOR TOWARDS THE MISSION

Some missions—The Attitude of the Poor towards the mission—
The Moral and Economical aspect of mission work- Its
patronage and publicity—Its parasites and abuse—Natural
law of debtor and creditor between the Poor and the mission.

WE have dealt already with the religious and educative missions, but of the making of missions there is
no end. Philanthropy being sympathetic suffering, the
Rich are not in the habit of submitting without an effort
to any kind of suffering, sympathetic or otherwise, and
so each time they suffer through the distress of the Poor
they have to invent a new mission, on the ground that
the numerous existing missions are still insufficient for
their protection. When we are gazing upon a fire, and
suddenly see the movement of a figure in the upper flat,
retreat by the stair cut off, and the escape too short to
reach the window, it is our own agony to which we
give expression when we ask, Can nothing be done?
Can no one do anything? Or, gazing at the ship upon
the rocks, the few remaining sailors being washed from
the rigging one by one, and there is no help near, no
lifeboat, no rocket apparatus, it is our own unendur-

able anguish that asks, Is there no help? Can we not do anything to save them? Once find that "anything," no matter what it is, and our weakness and sufferings disappear in action. The doomed sailors suffer as they have suffered, but our burden is dissipated in hope of relief and help. From great things to small, that is exactly how it is with the philanthropist. When he sees a poorly-clad woman, an apparently starving man, or neglected child, his cry at once is, Can nothing be done? Cannot we do something? Existing agencies having permitted such a thing to exist, we must start a new one. Thus it is our inability to endure the sufferings of the Poor that is the mainspring of all missions. Whether the Poor can endure their own sufferings without much distress, we do not seek to inquire; to the true philanthropist it would not matter if they could, it would not relieve his distress. Only removing it out of sight would satisfy him, and for that purpose he requires a mission. Thus, at the very initial stage of his operations, he may be organising an institution for the relief of what does not exist; for if the Poor do not suffer from their appearances of distress, of what use is the mission? More or less this element of exaggeration is in all missions, because of the difference of pain-endurance between the Rich and the Poor.

All purely relieving missions, although they differentiate as to their form of relief—some confining themselves to children's clothes, some are dorcas-missions, some medical dispensaries—are the same in principle and general character. They advertise to the whole city what they have to dispose of; and as their success depends, not upon the careful guardianship of the material in their charge, that it should be only used for the purposes for which it was intended, but upon the amount they can get rid of in a given time, such a thing as confining themselves to genuine cases is a myth. Were they to do so they might put up their shutters, and shut their door in a week for want of occupation, and in some cases need not have begun at all. That those institutions whose success depends upon how many useful articles they can give away are not more successful, is a high compliment to the sturdy independence of the poorer classes. If they opened their stalls on the same condition among some of the shabby-genteel sections of society they would be better appreciated. As it is, it is never the really poorest class who patronise the mission, the class for whom the mission was created, but the people who are one or two social steps above them, people on the verge of respect-ability and who would be compelled to purchase that great emblem of respectability, clothes, if they could not get them for nothing.

These relieving missions, however, beyond breeding a class of parasites, not of the Poor, do not do much harm. They delude their subscribers that they are "doing something" for the Poor, and their feelings are relieved from suffering their distress : they afford some excellent opportunities for the busybodies—but non-subscribers—to air their oratory at the annual meet-ings, and to pass a number of votes of thanks, among which is one to the officers, two or three snugly-paid individuals whose interest is not to let the institution go down. Like hotels among the Rich, the Poor will get to know where these institutions are located, if they should want them, and perhaps a genuine case of distress may occasionally find them useful.

So generally acknowledged is it that these missions are as incapable of protecting themselves from being taken advantage of, as they are of discharging the duties entrusted to them without depending upon a great many people who have no interest in them but

what they can get from them, that when a new one is
spoken of, or an old one recommended, stress is put
upon the means they have of ferreting out and succour-
ing cases of genuine distress. Now by the laws of
Nature distress is pain, and pain is weakness, and every
living thing desires to hide its weakness and display its
strength ; and these distressing cases among the Poor
that are wormed out are cases where the Poor have
preferred bearing their troubles by themselves in secret,
rather than expose them, even for the relief they knew
the mission would afford them. There is more good
to humanity in a person bearing his own troubles in
silence than in all the virtues ; and this exceeding good
that all Nature strives for is destroyed and trampled
upon by this gimlet-and-keyhole searching for genuine
distress. If genuine distress does not seek relief, it
does not wish to exchange its secret for succour, and
its wishes ought to be respected. But among the Poor
the missioner and his satellites have no respect for
privacy or domestic decency ; a case of genuine distress
is a rare prize in a host of blanks, to be told in triumph ;
reported in the newspapers ; and the reward of the
brave victim is not only to have his secrecy destroyed and
his weakness laid bare, but to have the fact made public
all over the country. A neighbour of one of these heroes
tells the visitor of the mission, he does not think all is
right with So-and-so, and the visitor (male or female)
is all alert at once. The door of the victim is knocked
at and entrance demanded, searching and most personal
questions as to his or her last meal, and of what it con-
sisted, as to their present state of funds, their prospects
of another meal, &c., are put as if the victim was on his
or her oath. Without permission, the larder, the wardrobe
(what stands for these in a single room), and every
part of the house is searched, as if for stolen goods.
Soon under this pressure weakness breaks down reso-

lution, and the whole truth comes out ; then the victim
is carried in triumph to the mission, his feeling of shame
and disgrace outweighing all the good fifty missions
could do him. But then his story, pathetically dressed
for publication, makes the fountains of charity flow ;
and no matter what the mission, or what its purpose,
the fountains of charity must be its first concern.
" Butchered to make a Roman holiday," and the fibre
of resolution and endurance that was growing so finely
is destroyed, perhaps for ever ! Better be a mission
parasite than the victim of a " genuine case of
distress," to be advertised all over the country.

The moral and economic aspects of these missions
are not so harmless.

If a mission takes upon itself to clothe a man's child
while the man is too indifferent to do so adequately
himself, he will let it, and be thankful for the relief.
But he will in future arrange his finances without
setting aside any provision for the clothing of that
child. No matter how little money he was earning
when the mission took the child, or how much more
he may earn afterwards, he will never have money
enough for that child's clothing. It has ceased to be
part of his economy. For whatever purpose, moral or
immoral, he spends his wages, the mission increases
his spending power by relieving him of part of his
obligations.

The habit of a great many, perhaps the majority, of
the lowest class of wage-earners is, after paying such
debts as they cannot escape, and making the lowest
provision for the coming week (as they cannot be
trusted), to spend their money in drink and other things
on Saturday night—every penny of it. Does the mission that provides Sunday breakfasts help these people
to learn a better and more provident use of their
money, or by its aid help them to still further reduce

the amount they set aside, and leave more for the saturnalia? The law of Nature is that man can only pass to a better state by pain. All the benefactors of mankind have only been able to protect their fellow-men from evil, or warn them to avoid it, by their personal experience of it. When a person can endure the results of his actions he is hard to convince of their vice, but when he cannot, he requires no other conviction than his own experience. If a person spends in one day the money that was to provide food for the following six, there is the starvation of these six to teach him better next time; but if a mission relieves him of the suffering of his own act, where is the educative element to come from, when the individual is beyond the resources of religion?

But there are some missions less harmless than these—missions to provide the poor with pleasures they of themselves can never hope to attain, but once enjoyed, leave them either with a feeling of discontent at the limitations of their own lives, or a strong desire to imitate these pleasures without adequate means, and so increase their poverty and improvidence.

By the laws of their caste, the upper crust of society is forced to live a very peripatetic form of life. They have to be in London during the season. They have to go out of town somewhere, when it is over. They have to go to the moors in August for the shooting. They have to be at home for Christmas. They have again to come to town in February for the opening of Parliament, then go off to the Mediterranean in spring, and again return for the season. And according to our means, for our means generally denote our leisure, by the laws of Imitation we all follow this plan as far as we can, down to the middle classes who can only afford a holiday of a month or so, each summer, at coast or country. Such a perambulatory life teaches the eye to habituate itself to great variety of colour, change of scenery, and greater diversity and movement in life. Monotony and sameness in anything becomes unendurable.

A person trained to this life goes down among the Poor in their native quarter. He is less interested in their physical condition than their surroundings. He cannot endure the monotony of grey in their houses and streets ; his eye is offended with the regularity of the architecture of the street, its sameness, lack of colour, and absence of ornamentation. The houses are high, the streets narrow, and he says there is no Sun, and he cannot breathe for want of air. He thinks the Poor feel all these things as he does. He declares that what the Poor require is their lives brightened up a bit ; he says they are longing for sunshine and fresh breezes, for flowers and scenery, and to hear the birds sing ; and of course for this purpose they must have a mission.

Now the eye of everybody, town dweller or peripatetic, is formed in regard to colour, motion, and variety by his environment, and the town dweller can no more sigh for the environment of the country, which he has never seen, than he would for the coronation robes of King Cophetua. He may have some knowledge of both, and a curiosity to see them, but he suffers no loss for want of them. The writer is born of the street streety, and notwithstanding some years of roving, finds a more restful pleasure to the eye in a street than anywhere else. He has consulted hundreds of a similar training, and their experience is all the same. He never sees the sun, and for sunshine his object is to get out of it if too warm, or get into it when balmy and temperate. He walks the street every day of his life, his eyes never rising above the level of his own sight. He sees the street and the pavement, the shops and the passers-by, but he could not tell you what like the upper story of a house is that he passes every day. Like the sun, it is beyond his line of vision unless at a distance. This is the experience of the great bulk of the industrial classes of a town, and sometimes they are nine tenths of the whole inhabitants.

Of course it is not the Poor who benefit by these excursion missions, whether they are single day, week-end, or fortnightly ; they are of all these. To go out of town requires that essential of respectability—clothes, and the Poor have not got them. But the family of the well-paid workman have, and go as substitutes for their poorer brethren. It is a great relief to the workman, as otherwise he would require to pay for their holiday himself.

Some of these excursionising missions confine their operations to children. They can always have the children of the Poor for nothing, but they have first to clothe them ; after that they can keep them as long as they like. What effect these holidays have upon the little things, unless that of a little healthfulness, we do not know. They are irresponsible beings upon whom effects exhaust themselves, and do not pass to the community. But where the mission is not one of selection and favour, there is plenty of rivalry, sycophancy, deceit, and lying, upon the part of parents to get their children included in the favoured number, and an ill-natured grunt when they are returned upon their hands again.

There is more sympathy, sentiment, and tears can be spent over children in an hour than over adults in a week, and yet children are born with the natural power of making their own enjoyment. They require neither change, nor toys, nor company. Like the lamb, the puppy, or the kitten, their pleasure comes from within themselves, and if they can find nothing near them to play with, they can chase their own tails.

From the occasional trip to the country, to the reposeful case of Convalescent Homes is but a step. One would think from its name that a Convalescent Home was an adjunct or extension of a hospital, under strict medical superintendence. But in many towns such is not the case. Were such the case all the subscriptions would go to the hospital, and all the credit would go to the hospital's board of directors. Perish the thought! Are there not poor people who nurse their sickness at home, but have not the means to get the necessary change of air during convalescence? And, therefore, shall we not build a convalescent home of our own for these poor people? Shall we not have fashionable bazaars with nobility at the stalls? Shall we not have laying of foundation stones, and building of wings, and all with the necessary amount of fulsome flattery, mutual admiration, resolutions, and champagne luncheons.

These voluntary institutions are made to be abused, are abused, and are known by everybody to be abused. Like every other voluntary institution, these Homes depend for their success upon their occupation. To keep fully occupied, to show the need every now and then of extension, to read at the annual meeting the same old report with the same stupid figures about how many have enjoyed its advantages, and the usual deficit, is all that an institution of this kind requires to keep it upon the broad road of prosperity. Who the people are who board and lodge in these caravans, it is best not to ask. They are a set of professional loafers, who go from one to another with all the ease of honoured guests. They know the proper forms by which to apply for admittance, with all the necessary recommendations, and when is the best time for application. These institutions being governed by amateurs, who mistake elaboration of form for the true spirit of business, are saturated with red tape and formula, and it is only these loafers who study all their forms. The regularity

of your form of application is of more importance
than the desperation of your case. These institutions
cannot keep empty while the workman is recovering
from sickness, and would require their services. They
must fill their wards with whoever comes, and when
the true case appears they have no room for him,
unless he can wait until they have another bazaar and
build a new wing for him.

A lady informed the writer that although she subscribed to every mission in connection with her church
and social circle, and her husband, from his counting-
house, subscribed to every public institution that was
voluntarily supported, she had callers in one week to
the number of twenty-five soliciting for missions from
half-a-crown to one pound. The writer informed her
that it was only because the other fifty or so did not
know her address, or that their collectors were engaged
elsewhere, that she escaped a visit from them also.
With one or two rare exceptions all of these are
voluntary institutions, with no check of any kind upon
them, no responsibility for their stewardship to any
person. They are all begotten of vanity and the influence
" running a mission " has in social circles. They are all
highly sentimental, because they are meant for talking
and not work, and their principal aim is to shed glory,
admiration, and envy upon their principals. It may be
safe to say, that as regards the Poor they are all useless
and utterly idiotic. Some are to encourage the Poor to
window-sill floriculture, as if the Poor had not enough to
do already. Some want to encourage their taste for art
by presenting them with approved oleographs. Others
want to teach the women how to make their own
clothes, forgetting that all but the house-mother are
out at work all day, and having earned rest and leisure
for the evening have no intention to give it up to
renewed labour. And the house-mother must have

been expected to have a dual existence if she could cook for her family, do the work of the house, and attend to her children, and at the same time study paper patterns, or learn to work the sewing-machine.

A few matrons connected with a fashionable church were grieved to hear that the female Poor wore their underclothing without repair until they were done with, and then bought new ones. These ladies had large houses, servants, sewing-machines, and, when required, seamstresses. At every washing the family linen was carefully gone over, stitched, and repaired, and they therefore knew the value of the proverb "a stitch in time." It vexed and astonished them to learn that the Poor not only did no repairing, but did not know how, even the mysteries of plain-sewing being beyond them. The mission was at once started. It was announced from the churches, circulated in the mission halls, and advertised in the local papers that the Poor would be taught the making of underwear, that all material would be provided gratis, and sewing-machines and teachers would be in attendance. When the doors were opened on the first night, in there walked—whom? The daughters of the Poor? Not one of them; but about a dozen demure young ladies, respectably dressed. They were warehouse girls, whose situations depended upon their maintaining a certain standard of respectability in clothes. These young ladies had a strong suspicion that they would get the made articles home with them— the articles cut and made by the teachers—which turned out true, and these were very useful to them. But they soon showed that their interest was centred in the outer, not the under, garments, which they treated with the same contempt as their poorer sisters. How to alter, clean, and renovate dress was what was asked—and the mission closed.

It was not safe to speak about that mission to any

of these matrons for months afterwards. They simply
snorted with indignation and anger at what they called
the ingratitude of the Poor. They never thought any
blame attached to themselves in not having first consulted the Poor to see if their purpose was desirable or
feasible. Such a condescension was beneath them.
Anybody might be glad of the offer they made, &c.,
&c. Yet strange to say, the people specially singled
out to receive this great blessing were not glad ; if
anything, were uninterested and unmoved.

The attitude of the Poor towards all these missions—
towards missions of all kinds but the giving kind—is
one of indifference and contempt. The principal reason
for this is that in the eyes of the Poor every mission is
steeped in patronage and condescension. Nor can this
be otherwise, from the nature of Social Law. Every
social seam must patronise the seams below it, to show
the line of demarcation between them. There is
nothing that gives a philanthropist of the middle
classes a right to tell his poorer brother how he
should live but his social position ; and all he has to
tell him is patronage—" what we do " ; and what we
do is right. Yet a person living a social flight or two
above the philanthropist patronises him in the very
same way. Many of the habits of the two classes are
different, and he tells the philanthropist it is only
" what we do " is right. Why should a lord or bishop
be listened to with more respect than an ordinary
person ? Yet we know that they are. Why should a
well-dressed man think he has a right to be listened
to by a workman ? It is not what is said at missions
—all of that the Poor have heard a thousand times—it
is how it is said. You are not living as *we* should wish
you. Your habits are offensive to *us*. You would find
it much better for yourselves if you would do as *we*
advise you ; and so on. This patronage is infinitely

worse when it is ladies who are evangelising. Men are governed in their actions generally by their business instincts, because their business hours are their intensest; but women are wholly social in thought, intent, and deed, and the patronage is laid on with rigour. The self-consciousness of a woman is never laid aside. She always knows who she is, and who she is speaking to, and in her conversation she thinks less of using words that are convincing in themselves than of words that should be convincing because she has said them. The instinct in every woman to let whatever woman she comes in contact with "know her position" never dies. It is not an intention always to humiliate, but an inherent weakness that knows not how else to assert itself. This is very plainly seen in what are called reclaiming missions. It is a pity that men do not reclaim: they have their businesses to attend to, and so it is left to women and those men who are ultra-feminine by nature. If men reclaimed, their business habits would keep them from too much intercourse with the culprit. There would be no upbraiding, and no conscious superiority. They would assure the unfortunate by their action, rather than by speech, that the whole case was understood, and need not again be referred to. They would tell him, with no more superiority than must always exist in one who has orders to give, what was required of him, and leave him in peace to fulfil it. But the female reclaimers have a very different way of going about things. They never fail to let the Magdalen know the difference between them; they have not the courage to sympathise with her, for fear of being thought to sympathise with her life; they keep marking their horror of her past by a frigidity and distance from her person that is both painful and humiliating to the victim. They show her in every action that she may become reclaimed,

but will never be allowed to become one of them.
"What use, then, submitting to all this indignity?"
says the victim ; "better a thousand times back to my
old life, with all its evils and hardships. There, at
least, are friendship and sympathy ; there none can
cast a stone at me." Of all missions the reclaiming is
the stupidest and most useless, but of course hugely
sentimental. And of all people most incapable for the
work are the ladies who gush about it being peculiarly
women's work, because of their womanly sympathies,
their warm hearts, that know too well what women's
trials are, &c., &c. Among women there are only two
classes—the virtuous and the other kind ; and when a
woman sins she knows there is no social redemption.
The pure will not have her, whether she gives up her
old life or not, and there is no middle class. She
cannot stand alone, and she must have companionship
and sympathy. No wonder these Magdalen institutions have generally to catch their victims at the prison
gate.

The prison-gate mission for men stands upon a
different platform ; there is here no insuperable social
barrier, and men are strong enough to be able to
sympathise with criminals without being suspected of
criminal tendencies ; they are also strong enough to
treat a person kindly without sympathising with his
career. Yet the principle of the mission is as sentimental as it is wide of the facts. The idea that all
young people who are in prison are anxious when they
come out of being saved from their companions is
imaginative, but nothing more. It implies that the jail-
bird is always innocent, and his companions criminal,
and only waiting his release to tempt him again to be
their catspaw. Such a condition of things is the stock
property of the novelist and "The Ticket-of-leave-
Man " ; but it is a poor compliment to the police, or

the innocent-guilty party himself. If the police can never catch anybody but an innocent, it is a pity; and if an innocent finds he has been entrapped, why does he not denounce his colleagues? The facts are generally these: if a jail-bird is of the criminal classes he wants to get back to his friends as soon as he is released. There, and there only, the fatted calf is killed for him. Generally they are at the gate waiting for him. If he be not of the criminal classes and has got into trouble through misfortune—his own or another's—when he gets out he wants to get back to his family or friends. There only is sympathy and privacy. Should his offence be too great for society to tolerate him again, then long before his release, preparations have been made for his emigration. That man does not want to see any prison-gate mis- sioner. No person with friends requires the services of a mission. Who, then, is friendless and criminal? It is a rare and unnatural combination. Everybody in jail, whether innocent, criminal, or friendless, has thought out the question long before his release what he shall do when he gets out, and in his plans there are no thoughts of prison missions unless to take advantage of them. It may be objected here that we have left no room for repentance. Remorse and repentance for criminal acts are strongest when the prisoner is in the dock receiving his sentence. It is then the full force of his act comes home to him; *then* the difference between his position and that of the law-abiding is most strongly impressed upon him. The calm re- flection of a few months in jail effaces wholly or in part this feeling; intense impressions are not durable. The culprit gets to think of his action as from the stand- point of a neutral party, and his mind is fixed upon the future and how to repair his fallen fortunes. If he intends continuing his career, he is not likely to tell

any one ; if he intends to reform he is less likely to
begin the process with a few strangers who will advertise the fact.

With a large submerged tenth who are voluntarily
living the lowest form of city existence, there is no
benevolent mission of any kind they cannot turn to
account. Every mission that gives a bed or breakfast,
a bath or a pair of boots, is offering to them a higher
mode of life than their own ; always an attraction if
unaccompanied with too much of the *quid pro quo*, labour
or restraint. Therefore, no matter how sentimental the
mission may be, it can always be sure of an intermittent patronage sufficient to make a report. But
that there is not the slightest intention of these patrons
to reclaim themselves or in any way alter their habits
is perfectly well known. The philanthropist is content
with so very little in the way of promise of redemption
that he not only meets his poor halfway, but goes himself all the way. He so keeps before his mind the ideal
side of his mission, that he does not like to think any one
could possibly come for the lures and bribes ; therefore
when a person seeks his mission he convinces himself
that it is for its healing springs. Undeceived a thousand times he retains his faith and conviction with the
tenacity of despair ; to accept the truth would be to
prove his mission a failure. The only defence he has
is to charge the Poor with deception and ingratitude.

On behalf of the Poor we say the charge is not well
founded, and we only notice the subject because it is
the most popular defence of mission failure.

Mission philanthropy, as we have said elsewhere, is
sentimental, that is, it is without reason, without
knowledge, without regard to the laws of Nature,
economy, or causation. Commercial or practical men
are afraid to examine and discuss philanthropical

schemes in the same business-like way they would
trade affairs. If they did, every one of the mission
schemes would be condemned, or so modified as to
take all the beautiful sentiment out of them; and to
condemn philanthropy in its wildest aspect, that is, its
most sentimental, is to be pilloried as an enemy to
progress and a hinderer of the elevation of the masses;
something suggestive of being irreligious and immoral.
But although philanthropy is so superior to ordinary
law it demands a very exact fulfilment of all the laws
and prophets towards itself. This is necessary from
its inherent weakness. A sentiment is like nothing
else in the world, and to be successful requires all and
sundry connected with it to act towards it on a higher
plane of virtue, than exists anywhere. That is the
reason they remain sentiments—or failures. The
Poor do not see the sentiment of a mission, and if they
did would leave the people of the mission to carry out
their sentiment themselves, because the Poor do not
govern their lives by sentiment. What they see in the
mission, is a number of the better classes come voluntarily among them to get them to change their mode
of life. They have made no compact with these
gentlemen, they have undertaken no obligation expressed or implied. If the mission be a purely
teaching one, they are not likely to come much in
contact; but if the mission offers gifts, they may have
occasion for these gifts. Without caring what the
mission thinks, or wishes, or understands, they follow
the Natural law that governs the whole world under
the circumstances—even philanthropists—they resolve
to pay as little for them as they can. If they have to
sing a hymn, or endure a sermon for what they want,
they do so if it is worth it, and they cannot escape
the infliction, and they consider then the bargain finally

closed. But when they are told that for a temporary relief, say a dinner or a pair of boots, they are expected to come every night afterwards to be prayed over or sermonised, they wonder what manner of man he is who expects so much for so little, and if he deals in such a generous manner in his own affairs. To attempt to establish an equivalent between a temporary obligation and a perpetual one, would be repudiated by the reason of a child ; and to expect that for an overcoat or blanket a person is going to change the habits of a lifetime, going to adopt a new set of habits for the rest of his life, is as unreasonable. The Poor pay what they have to pay to the mission for what they get, and their consciences are clear. The charge of deceit is technically correct, but it is a form of deceit universally practised, and not even the missioner can cast a stone. The wife can only gratify her wishes through her husband. When she wants him to give her something, she seeks to make herself a *persona grata* to him. She is more affectionate, more considerate, studies more than usual his tastes, his comforts, and his inclinations, and when she has won him into his best humour, proffers her request. Of course she was deceiving him. So little however does she think of her moral obliquity that she prefers this manner to straightforward asking. The daughter in like manner cajoles her father with bursts of duty and professions of love that come to an end after the request is granted. She is deceiving him just the same as the Poor deceive the mission. Every person who has a desire, studies the easiest and most certain way of getting it, and if it can only be got through another person, his help, or consent, the first thing is to propitiate him. Instances are too numerous to quote, as the principle runs through nearly every action of our daily life.

It is the fault of the better classes, and the philanthropist more than any other person, that the Poor can get nothing from or through the Rich unless under promise of moral regeneration. That is the unchangeable condition on which the better classes will lift a finger to help the Poor. We cannot spend fifty years denouncing their immoral lives, their thriftlessness, their drunkenness, and their irreligion, and then supply them with the means of continuing them. As well expect a teetotaller to comply with the request of a drunkard to give him money to continue his debauch. Therefore when the Poor require the services of the mission, they seek them through the only way that is open to them ; nor need the missioners be deceived by their protestations any more than the father is by his daughter's blandishments, if it were not that they are wholly absorbed in the pleasing imagination of having caught a convert.

There is an underlying perpetual warfare between the teacher and the pupil. The latter wants to acquire his knowledge in the natural way, by experience and imitation ; the former, by the civilised process of precept only. In other words, we educate our people upon the plan : It is not what you wish to know, but what we wish you should know. Such a system can only be carried out where there is some authority to enforce it. If we did not teach our children while they were under our authority, they would only learn what they wished to know. Such is the position between the mission and the Poor. We are desirous that they should learn, and are industriously teaching them one half of our lives only, the religious and the moral half, the self-denying, self-repressing, self-sacrificing, anti-pleasure half. They are busy ruining themselves imitating the other half of our lives, the ease-giving, pleasure-giving, self-indulgent, enjoyable half ; and as long as we cannot make our own lives a whole, an indivisible whole, of virtue and happiness combined, the Poor will follow their natures and continue to imitate the happiness only.

CHAPTER X

A SENTIMENTAL MISSION

A sentimental mission— A personal experience that explains
itself.

THE writer was sitting one afternoon in one of the
wards of a large city hospital. I was visiting an old
friend, a woman, who had just gone through a very
painful and dangerous operation. She had struggled
with her ailment, as most women do, for a long time in
private, but its recurrence, more painful and debilitating
each time, at shorter and shorter intervals, at last compelled her to submit herself to medical treatment.
Her physician had a reputation as a gynæcologist, and
no doubt treated her as skillfully as he could, but after
a time he informed her that nothing could save her
but an operation, an operation by no means common
nor always successful. The doctor impressed thoroughly
upon his patient the dangerous nature of the operation,
and left it to herself to decide whether she would risk
it, or live on in continuous pain, without hope of re-
covery or almost of alleviation. The woman's outlook
was not a happy one. Weakened mentally and physically with pain, she had hardly the strength of mind
to come to any decision. When her sufferings were

great, any relief, no matter how doubtful or dangerous, seemed to her welcome ; when they passed for the moment, the dread of a fatal termination frightened her back into the old submission and endurance. Her friends however got her coaxed to submit to surgical treatment, and for this purpose she must go to the hospital. Her physician arranged all the details of her removal ; promised to call upon her when in the hospital, and to be present at the operation, so that she would not be in the hands of strangers altogether.

After she had agreed to submit herself, she wrote for me to call and see her, and when I did so she asked me if I would promise to call and see her in the hospital, and in the event of things taking an unfavourable turn, discharge her wishes. For family reasons—the usual family bickerings—she had determined to place her affairs in the hands of an outsider, one who could have no interest beyond the discharge of an obligation he had voluntarily taken upon himself. For the purpose of private conversation the doctor got us the privilege of one hour per week, on a different day from the regular visitors' days.

The afternoon I speak of, was either my first or my second visit after the operation had been performed. The operation, so far as it left the patient still living, was successful, but as the woman had been over an hour upon the demonstrating-table, they had allowed her to catch cold, and pneumonia set in. In her weakened and fevered condition this nearly proved fatal. However, when I visited her she was slowly recovering, but very weak.

A very quiet subdued ward was this one for female patients. A hall of about fifty feet long by twenty-five or so broad, with a corresponding high roof, and tall narrow windows on both sides at regular intervals. Between the windows were the cots, about eight or nine

on either side, and each cot had its patient. The swing-
ing doors at the two ends swung noiselessly, and as the
floor was covered with deadening matting in the centre
one knew not who entered or left unless by watching the
door. There was no conversation between the occu-
pants ; the distance between their cots made conversation difficult, because the slightest raising of the voice
echoed throughout the ward, and frightened them.
The silence laid its gentle influence upon us all, and it
came natural to us to talk in undertones. When the
nurses came to attend to a patient, to diet or dress
her, it was done in silence, and the conversation went
on in whispers. When the doctor appeared to speak
to the nurses, it was in a low undertone, and the little
Bible-reader—the only other stranger beside myself—
flitted from cot to cot in silence and spoke in whispers.

I had but just come in, and had taken my seat in
the usual position, facing the patient and with my back
towards the door. We had only spoken a few words
when there burst upon us suddenly and without
warning the most horrible noise it was ever my fate
to listen to. It was not a yell, a scream, or a shout,
but a sustained strident noise, like a steam-pipe escape.
Such for an instant was the effect upon my unsuspect-
ing jarred nerves that I ducked my head between my
shoulders as if to escape a blow, and in this position
ere two or three seconds passed I knew what the
matter was—it was some ladies singing hymns. I did
not look round—I did not require to—I did not wish to.
I felt an anger surging in my heart to which it had been
a stranger for years. I looked at my patient. It was
not the expression of resignation she gave me at finding our precious hour destroyed by this interruption,
but the distress evidenced in every line of her face at
her inability to hide the torture the singing was inflicting
upon her, under a sense of religious duty. The cot next

to her was surrounded by a folding screen : the woman was dying. Further down was the little Bible-reader of whom I have spoken, talking to a patient. I had met her in the ward before, and was particularly struck by her method of working, it was so gentle, so worldly-wise, and so successful. Knowing the prejudice the Poor have to be bibleised, she kept her book well under her arm as she entered. She would go quietly to a cot, sit down and talk to the patient. The subject was always the patient's self, and her affairs. The Bible-reader had found out that that was the quickest way of interesting them. She talked about their home, their family, their ailment, &c. "Could she do anything for them?" and when she had got them to open their hearts to her, then came the request, "Might she not read a little to them?" More than once I had watched with amusement and curiosity, the scene. The patient pillowed up to a sitting position, reading or knitting. When the attack began the conversation went on, and so did the knitting. By and by the knitting stopped and the hands were still : then the work fell from the idle fingers, or was gathered up and put away. After that we looked for the Bible to come out of its hiding-place. But what she read was for the ear of the patient only ; the cot next to them must not be disturbed, she might not be attuned for reading, and even the Bible can be as distressing as the Devil's Tarantelle when the mind is the prisoner of the body's pain. The little reader had to attune all her subjects herself, and some-times after all they refused her request. They were too distraught with other things to control their thoughts. On this occasion the reader had just opened her Bible when the singing began. The pained expression upon her face as she realised that all her work had gone for nothing, as only a fog-horn could have been heard above the din of the music, was vexing to see ; nor

need she wait any longer ; not *that* day again would the
nerves of these poor and helpless creatures be calmed
sufficiently for thought or reflection.   She rose and left.

Some of the other patients had been sleeping, and
the expression of dread and amazement with which
they tried for a moment to understand what awoke
them would certainly not help their convalescence.
Others, again, after listening for a minute or two,
turned their backs upon the singers and covered their
heads with the bedclothes.   One poor girl, with a face
like a frightened deer, looked as if they had come to
upbraid her, and her alone.   Whether they were looking at her I could not say, but her startled look suggested that they were.   Evidently the suddenness of
their attack had wrenched her mind back upon some
tender past, because after looking for some means of
escape, and finding herself at bay, in desperation she
attempted to join them in their hymn.   Her lips moved
spasmodically, but no sound came.   Two or three only
of all the patients showed any interest in the performance—that is, they sat up in bed with that respectful
attention the Poor invariably assume towards their
betters in religious matters.

The writer has been a musical enthusiast all his life,
and he has given years of study to it, especially vocal
music and voice-production.   It was therefore no
trouble to him to know without looking round that
there were only two singers—females—and that they
were neither young nor beautiful.   Their voices were
pitched in a higher key than their natural timbre, and
to sustain the pitch they had to yell without any control over the voice whatever.   This constant straining
had produced a harsh, hard tone, without a particle
of sympathy or softness, that was exceedingly nerve-
piercing.   There was no attempt at modulation, light
or shade, nor observance of the nuances suggested by

either words or music. They were as even in tone
all through as a steam-whistle. I had heard the same
voices in many female music-hall singers, who had
spent their lives in contending with discordant and
unruly orchestras ; but the voice is most frequently
the product of congregational singing—congregational
singing of the worst kind, where everybody shouts
louder than her neighbour so as to hear her voice
come back to her above the din. They started a
second hymn after the first, without stoppage or break
of any kind. It was evident they were discharging
a duty—and one that required something of an
effort—and that so much of this discordant horror
must be poured on the lacerated nerves of these poor
patients.

The writer's mood had changed from anger to a deep
sorrow. He knew these young ladies were victims to
somebody's idiotic sentiment, and that they were acting,
perhaps, under a deep sense of religious conviction.
Then, he turned, as his custom is, to self-accusation.
Why, he asked of himself, must everybody associate
age and ugliness with whatever actions they dislike ?
Why should these ladies not be young ? How should
they not be beautiful ? Many young ladies have un-
musical voices ; plenty of pretty girls cannot sing any
better than these. It is true, I answered myself, we
always attribute *all* the vices to the person in whom
we find *one* we dislike ; but in this case the thing is
different. In hopes that I was wrong, and in justice to
the ladies, I turned round to look at them. Two ladies
past the first and past the second bloom of youth,
standing together upright as pillar-boxes, and as
motionless, with hymn-books open before them, faces
as expressionless as sphinxes, and with no more
movement than was necessary to sing, were looking
straight ahead of them, and pouring out their hymns

without caring what effect they had on any person. The taller of the two was above the middle height : every line of her face and figure denoted resolution. The face, like most resolute faces, was square and flat : there was not a soft or rounded line about it. It had no cheek, it had no chin, it had no lips—all these had long since been absorbed in muscle, and the muscles lay firm as whipcord beneath the skin. She looked a person who was capable of doing a duty without being able to enter into the spirit of it, and in following the letter of it would care little for the effects it produced on others. The other lady was not so tall, but would be considered tall when standing alone. She was a modified version of her friend, but looked as if she was not yet capable of doing without the support of her friend's stronger nature. She had not the features that had ever been beautiful, but had the appearance of one who, conscious of Nature's lack of gifts, determined to be noticeable for her willing services.

After the third hymn the ladies closed their books with a snap, turned upon their heels, and left the ward as abruptly as they had come. Whether they spoke to the nurses on coming in I cannot tell ; they spoke to no one when going away.

The abrupt change to the ordinary quietude again, made it by contrast an exaggerated stillness, and the intensity of the silence felt as if it was stronger than any of us could break, nor could we bring back our jangled thoughts to their usual groove. I fell into a reverie. I saw before me, as if it were a scene upon the stage of a theatre, a hall in connection with a church. On the platform was the clergyman of the church in the chair, supported by one or two other clergymen, some ladies, and two or three milk-cow philanthropists. The audience about half-filled the hall, they were mostly women—ladies connected with the church—but there was also a sprinkling of men, of whom the writer was one.

The meeting opened with the usual praise and prayer, and then the chairman introduced the purpose of the gathering and the principal speaker. The latter was a peripatetic evangelist who had a new and beautiful idea, and had honoured this particular church so highly as to give them the benefit of it first. In his introductory remarks the chairman dwelt much upon that as a great manifestation of God's goodness to them in choosing them for the good work.

Then the peripatetic unfolded his scheme. Everybody who has any acquaintance with religious philanthropy is aware of the extraordinary licence the speakers permit themselves. Gross exaggeration and improbability are so woven into scriptural quotations and Bible illustrations that from reverence for the latter we pass the other unchecked. On this occasion imagination ran riot. Nobody knew anything about the subject, and each speaker only sought to vie with his predecessors in glow of language and wealth of illustration. The audience grew quite enthusiastic, the writer among them.

Because that a repetition here of the inflated language used at the meeting would sound like mere blasphemy and burlesque, the writer does not use the words that are as well remembered to-day as the hour he heard them.

The speaker began by complimenting the city in its forward position in all good works. He mentioned several charities that had struck him as unique, and well worthy imitation by other towns. He remarked that there was a feeling abroad that the town was over-missioned, that their work conflicted and over-lapped ; but these were unworthy considerations to be put aside at once. There could be no arrest of the forces for good, no stoppage of the sacrifice we were willing to make for our neighbours' welfare. In such a mood he was thinking one day, not what already had been done for the Poor, or whether it was enough or too much, but what more could be done for them, and as he thought, suddenly an idea came into his head. (Of course he suggested by divine inspiration.) Looking over the vicissitudes in the life of the Poor, what was the most sorrowful and saddest part? Surely when overtaken by sickness they had to leave their homes, their children, the sympathy of friends, and enter the hospital! There, suffering and weak, strangers to each other, ruled by science, order, and silence, must they not long for the warm voices of sympathy and love! What then could we do to brighten the sad moments of the sick. It was not a case of material comfort; all that was medicinally provided for them. They were only temporary dwellers, and therefore it could not be a thing of a continuous nature; nor would it be well to be of a nature to require their co-operation or tire them. And having worked up a large catalogue of ineligibles, he unfolded his idea. What could be more comforting to them than to hear the old familiar hymns of their youth sung to them softly and sweetly by young, fresh voices? How it would draw their thoughts from their sufferings! How it would carry them back to the days of childhood when they sang these self-same tunes at their mothers' knee, or as they went and came in bands from Sunday-school! We all know the power that music has over the human heart, and if we planted here and there a hymn in the hearts of these poor stricken ones, might it not remind them that there is One on whom all suffering should be laid? Might it not even bring healing and comfort to the rebellious spirits who cannot recognise God's providence in pain? And so on.

And again—In what more appropriate service could the *divine* gift of music be spent than in the service of the Divine giver ? And surely in comforting the afflicted, we are engaged in His highest service. The gift of song is as rare as it is priceless ; its sway for good or evil over our emotions is almost unequalled. How seldom is it used to all the advantages for good it might be. Here is an opportunity that any musical young lady might embrace with enthusiasm, &c., &c.

As we have said, each speaker followed the other in the same strain, only trying to excel his predecessor in floweriness of language and imagination. Was there one of them all knew what he was talking about ; knew the ordinary working of a hospital, and yet believed in the feasibility of the idea? The writer was as full of enthusiasm as the others, but he had never been inside of a hospital. He knew accidents were taken there, and when he passed he saw people walking in the grounds in what seemed a state of convalescence. He had sang with others in asylums to the lunatics, in workhouses to the Poor, and in Convalescent Homes to the guests, and he thought this mission would run on similar lines. The singing would take place in a hall, and such as were strong enough and had the doctor's permission would be the audience.

The mission was formed, and because there was no need for male voices may be the reason the writer took no more interest in it.

When the singers had gone, I inquired who permitted such an outrage. " Does the resident doctor allow it ? " I asked. He said he had nothing to do with it. " But the professors," I said, " do they know of it, and do they ap-prove of it ? " " They have no power to stop it," was the reply. " What ! " I said, " the professors on the direc-torate, have they no power ? " " No ; they are outvoted

by the lay directors." Then came back to me, as it had
done many a time before, the omnipotence of the word
" Philanthropy." The lay members of such an important
public institution as a hospital would be men of credit and
renown in the city, and would almost assuredly be conspicuous for their religious observances. If one of these
was connected with the church that started the mission,
he dare not for his reputation refuse to see that permission was granted. Connected or not connected,
none of them if asked dare refuse their support. They
would be declared enemies of religion and philanthropy.
The professors had the fixing of the hour, and arranged
one when they were never there, an hour also at which
the lay director was winding up his business to go
home ; so the torture could go on without any of them
knowing the evil of it.

It rises to the lips of a reader almost naturally, that
the design of the mission and the carrying of it out were
two widely different things ; and if the original plan had
been fulfilled there is no reason to suspect that it would
not have had the effect so fondly imagined of it. That
if, instead of the singers who sang, there had been
young and fresh voices, the effect would have been
different. It is because of this difference between aim
and execution that the writer came to the conclusion
that all those who attended that meeting were as
ignorant of the ways and workings of a hospital as he
himself. The first visit he made to a ward would have
assured him, if he had been thinking about it, that such
an idea could not have been carried out, and if it could,
it would have done no good. Of all the missions the
writer has acquaintance with, this one required the
greatest courage in the performers. The mental strain
necessary to carry through such an unsympathetic task
was simply tremendous. What young ladies, up to
twenty-two years of age, not two, but say even four of

them, could go to a great building like a hospital, could move along its wide and echoing corridors making the only noise in the whole building, none speaking to them, or taking notice of them—as all had their own duties to attend to—turning into a ward like an empty hall, met there also by silence, and breaking out into song without preparing a single one of their audience.

We can conceive of young ladies going to an institution where they are waited for and welcomed, where with the encouragement of the staff they are brought to a ward, and allowed to go about and make the acquaintance of the patients, telling them what they intend to do, and asking them if they had any favourite hymn they would wish to hear. That, we imagine, young ladies might have the courage to do, if they could get over the depressing influence of the all-pervading quietude and the suggestive appearance of the still figures under the white sheets, or the meaning of the screens surrounding the cots. But that is an impossibility. Even if the staff were musically sympathetic themselves, what does that matter when most of their patients have been ordered rest and quietude ? And if the young ladies were allowed to fraternise in the ward as a preparation for their performance, they cannot sing to one alone, as the little Bible-reader could read ; then what about the others in the ward ? Though fifteen out of sixteen could have enjoyed the music, there must be silence if it is necessary for the health of the sixteenth. What professor would allow any young people to go into his ward and disturb his patients by talking to them—neither being friends of the patients, nor expected by them ? If the young people got speaking to the patients they would never open their mouths in song. Their sympathies would be too strong for them. They would see these poor people were suffering, that their thoughts were as far

from music or its endurance as from the cattle plague ;
they would see that to thrust music on these people
would be a distracting cruelty, and their courage would
fail them, and they would slip gently home and come
no more missionising.

It is strange how ready the philanthropist is to experiment upon the Poor. The belief in the therapeutic
virtues of music is old and common. Yet what person
of the better classes practises it upon his own sick ?
We walk the streets where the wealthy reside, and we
see straw laid down, and every loose thing about the
door wrapped in deadening cloths. Indoors everything
is quiet, and to be kept quiet for the patient's sake.
We have been in hundreds of the middle-class houses
where sick people lay. We have helped to chase away
barrel-organists and all other street musicians from the
neighbourhood. We have carried polite notes to the
neighbours requesting them to desist from all music-
playing and singing for the sick one's sake. Indoors
the piano or organ was shut, all musical instruments
put away, and everything in the shape of noise, musical
and otherwise, banished and suppressed. When we
are so careful to protect our own sick from its distracting noise, how can we imagine that it is good
for the sick Poor, or that they have any desire for it ?

What answer can be given to such a question ?
What other answer have we, than that in this country
philanthropy is accounted a special kind of righteous-
ness ? and as the " peripatetic " said, we cannot have too
much of it. It is true, the philanthropical and religious
classes cannot have too much of it ; but what about
the Poor ? Are they not to be considered ? It would
be all very well if these philanthropical people would
practise their ideas and sentiments upon their own paid
servants, so that the servants could leave when they
had had enough of it, or strike for higher wages when

the situation became oppressive.   Or upon their cattle,
or anything that was their own.   But philanthropy is
a very simple thing, with no room for sentiment or
religion about it.   It is merely the desire to help our
less fortunate fellow man ; and out of common courtesy
we should first make sure our interference with his life
and habits will be acceptable, and in what way our
services will be of use to him.   We *have* to do that
under similar circumstances to a person of our own
class ; why not to the Poor, when we are so anxious
to be of service to him ?

There is a defence ever upon the lips of the philanthropist when all others fail, and that is Good Intentions.   It is as much a justification for his folly as
" Didn't know it was loaded " is to the hero of a gun
tragedy.   It is best we should put plainly, for the
guidances of others, the limitation of such a defence.
When we are called upon to take action in any matter
of which we have neither knowledge nor experience, we
can only govern ourselves by good-intentions.   Because
of our ignorance we would rather not act at all, or get
some one of experience to act for us : failing that, we
must do the best we can ourselves.   And if our action
under such circumstances be not the best that could
have been done—be not even good—be positively the
very worst that could have been done—yet we have not
been wrong, because wrong implies a knowledge of
right : we have only been unfortunate in our good intentions.   But there is no justification in the world for
a person to act voluntarily, and at the same time act in
ignorance.   A voluntary act must be accompanied by a
perfect and intimate knowledge of all the details and
circumstances connected with everything affected by
it, and a positive knowledge that its results will be
beneficial and acceptable.   As there is no need to act
at all, so voluntary action is only justifiable by perfect

knowledge. What a world this would be if we were allowed to act towards each other as we do to the Poor ! Stop the machinery of a mill : interfere with the working of a coal-pit : reverse the engines of a locomotive : ruin men's businesses, and destroy their homes. All these things have occurred through voluntary interference combined with ignorance : all justified by good intentions ; but so signally condemned that we never hear of them now. Many bye-laws are in existence forbidding people to touch what they do not require to touch, whether from good or ill intentions.

That nervous unrest which besets so many of our philanthropists, as exemplified in the questions—What shall we do ? What is to be done next ? Can nothing be done ? finds great comfort in the text—" Do good : be ever doing good," as a mandate for their meddlesomeness. As a Christian admonition to all—that in the necessary actions of their lives there are few that cannot be made profitable to the community as well as to themselves—it is undoubtedly good advice. But it is not by any means the highest or safest guide to human actions. That is—" Do no evil." Follow that advice, and no matter how energetic or quiescent you choose to be in the world, the sum total of your actions is good—unalloyed good. But the thread of life is of such a mingled yarn, that follow the other plan, and the sum total of your actions may be for evil after all—even with the very best intentions. To act merely for the sake of doing good is folly and foolishness. There are many " goods " in every action, and many evils. It is better to do nothing than do wrong, no matter how sentimental the wrong may look.

It is the convalescent, not the sick, who can appreciate music, or desire it. As long as a person is really sick and suffering, all noises are distracting.

Quietude at that stage is always desired, not that it has any curative effect, but that it leaves the patient's mind wholly free from disturbance, to be devoted to his sufferings. Immediately the body is free from suffering, the mind returns to its normal condition ; returns before the body's strength returns, and with its return come back all the old desires—the longing for all the old habits and customs upon which the patient relied for his pleasures and enjoyment when in health. If music had been one of these, the patient would wish for it again ; but his desire for it would never be as strong as the smoker's longing for his pipe, or the tea-drinker's for her cup. Music ranks only among the second class of our desires, such as billiards and whist. If they can be had, so much the better ; but if not, they will neither constitute a lack nor create a yearning. The first-class desires are all personal—drink, smoke, tea, &c. The mind cannot long be diverted from them, nor will it accept any substitute for them.

CHAPTER XI

A NEW PHILANTHROPY

A new philanthropy —The weakness of the age cannot bear criticism—Without the initiative power to invent their own philanthropy—Self-improvement—Strength—What the poor have to do—What society has to do.

WE are informed by an authority that is not to be ignored, that no book dealing with existing methods is acceptable, unless it also contains a new plan. Destructive criticism, they say, is worthless unless accompanied by constructive forms of a new and attractive kind. That is, we must not find fault with anything, unless we are prepared to substitute some other thing in its place. It is an extraordinary commentary on the wisdom of this, the almost twentieth century, and the heir of all the gathered philosophy of its predecessors, that it is not to be told it is wrong, unless at the same time it is set right. It is content to go on in wrong if you have no other information for it. It is to do nothing for itself; it is not to stop and inquire; it is not to take warning, and seek new methods: the responsibility for all that must be upon the head of him who has found present systems faulty. What if his knowledge goes no further than to find Error without having found Truth? Then he is to remain silent.

When we see a man idly rowing on the river, should
we discover he is caught in the current of the falls,
unless we can also find a method for his safety we are
to be silent.   Our knowledge may go no further than
his danger : then let him go over the falls, boat and
all ; your remarks are only destructive criticism !
And this strange demand does not apply to science, to
philosophy, to economics ; it is principally confined
to social life and habit, and especially to philanthropy
—all actions that, if not voluntary, are mostly matters
of convenience.   Science surrenders its secrets slowly,
bit by bit, step by step, as if Nature said—"Digest
this slowly and thoroughly, then you will be in a fit
condition to appreciate the next step."   It may take a
hundred years before the man is born who finds out
that a hitherto accepted truth is false ; it may take
another hundred years to beget the man who finds out
what the truth is.   Would not the man who only discovered Error be held an enemy to mankind and science
if he kept his information to himself because he did not
discover Truth at the same time ?   How many scientific
questions have only got the length of the knowledge
of Error and are waiting patiently for the discoverer of
Truth !   So also in the business affairs of life, because
man is rational in business, being self-interested.   We
are continually finding old methods fail ; we can only
see where they are faulty ; we cannot find a cure
always for the fault.   Error and Truth do not grow
side by side, the one the complement of the other, like
the fabled bane and antidote.   Yet we are always glad
of what knowledge, no matter how small, we can get
about business concerns.   If we cannot avoid the
action we may at least strengthen its weak parts.
But in the unnecessary schemes of philanthropy we
must not cast out devils until we have gathered the
swine for their new tenancy.

The age has reached that stage of degeneration at which Rest is more feared than sought. The weak and overstrung nerves dread the approach of Rest as the drunkard fears sobriety, or the opium-eater the hour of disillusionment. From labour to labour, from excitement to excitement is endurable, but the thought of absolute idleness makes us shudder; against *that* civilisation must pile up safeguard upon safeguard. We must have books, music, theatres, dancing, everything and anything that will keep us from ourselves and from the dread *ennui* of Rest.

It is only the strong who are capable of enjoying rest; who can be with themselves as a friend; who can find their happiness within, and that do not require to borrow it from without; who can find pleasure in letting all their faculties lie fallow for a time, and feel content in the steady accumulation of new energy, repairing exhausted and worn tissue in brain and body, and driving away the clinging remnants of old excitement that hang to the nerves as tobacco-smoke to curtains. But the weaker we are the further we are from this peace, and the jaded, worn nerves that require rest most can least endure it. And of such are the philanthropical classes. It is their nervous dread of pain in any shape or form that makes them, or the most of them, philanthropists, and it is their craving for something new that makes them impatient of all criticism that does not carry with it a new excitement. The criticism is only endurable when hidden in the jam of a new method. And as children would prefer the jam without physic, so if our pages were all new philanthropical schemes they would be all the more welcome, though unaccompanied by a single reason why they should supplant the old.

We have been obliged to write the foregoing because we would have preferred laying down our pen at the

close of the last chapter. We thought that every
person who read these pages would wish to conduct
his philanthropy in future in his own way, guided by
his own experience and such of these lines that ap-
pealed to him as Truth. If diversity is the law of
Order, so is variety the father of Perfection. When
everybody brings together the fruits of independent
experience, then each can discard his own weak points
for his neighbours' stronger ones ; and by this constant
process of selection and rejection we may gather all
the best points together and weave them into a homo-
geneous and practicable whole. We have come, however, to depend so much upon Imitation as a guide to
our actions, that, like sheep, we are helpless and con-
fused without a leader. The more civilised we become ;
the more educated and the more refined, the more the
power of independent action is lost to us, and the more
we must depend upon Imitation. Nor is the leader
always the person who knows most about the subject ;
he may only be a person of stronger fibre than the
others, with sense enough to know what is the best
plan for himself, and power enough to put it into
execution. The loss of this power of initiative has
kept the world behind thousands of years in its
progress towards truth and knowledge. Instead of
Research marching on with the light and springy step
of Youth, encouraged and sustained by its tens of
thousands of worshippers, its feet are clogged and
chained to some cumbrous log to which all are clinging desperately. Not until it can shake off that log
will its feet be free, and then only to be fettered again
by some other.

How would it look, if when news was carried to a
village of the loss of a wayfarer, the villagers would
not go in search for him until some one among them
guessed where he might be ; then under this leader the

whole village sally forth to search in this one spot only.
Failing to find him there, they return to the village
until some other person makes a suggestion, and they
go forth again, and return again, and so on. The idea
that they should all scatter themselves, each taking a
different part, so that the whole neighbourhood may be
properly searched cannot occur to them, because they
have lost all power of initiative and have ceased to
trust in any thing that suggests individual action or
diversity of method. Just so it is with the philanthropist, he has no confidence in individual action. The
mission was in existence before him : it is the log to
which he has chained himself ; to think Philanthropy
by other means is beyond his capacity. The Poor, and
the world, must wait till the mission is dead before a
new step in philanthropy can be taken.

There is, however, one reason above the others why
we should have preferred leaving the making of plans
to those who delight in them, and that is, that in the
plan we present there is an almost fatal suggestion ;
a suggestion that has always been the most distasteful
and ungrateful that could be presented to a human
being—self-improvement   The reformer, as a general
rule, will undertake to reform anything upon earth but
himself. Only whisper self-improvement to him, and
the joy and the hope die out of his eyes ; his hands
fall idly by his side ; his enthusiasm turns cold to the
shivering point ; he finds it is not the game he meant
to play, and he can have no pleasure in it.

Divided as the Rich and Poor are from each other by
so many things, all antagonistic to any possibility of
co-operation, there is only one ground upon which they
can meet and work together for good and that is—
strength. Strength will cure all evils, it will banish
distress, it will defy misfortune, it will protect against
hunger, it will promote peace.

The Poor must be taught strength, and as their teachers are weaker at the present moment than they, their teachers must first cultivate it in themselves.

This is not a very pleasant outlook for the missioner. The equivalent for his services among the Poor, was the good opinion of the pious, and his own class,—one of the greatest social rewards one could find. That was the secret of the popularity of the mission. But in the new philanthropy the equivalent for services to the Poor will be the gratitude of the Poor, in proportion to success ; a very different and by no means equal reward. When the Poor send an imposing deputation of unemployed to the authorities demanding relief because they cannot find work, and when work is immediately offered to them at regulation rates, it is wonderful how soon that army melts into a corporal's guard of honestly intentioned men. The others found when the alternative was presented to them that it was relief, not work, they wanted. Let us hope our friends the philanthropists have not made the same mistake. They never cease from telling us that it is the love of the Poor, and that only, which inspires and sustains them in their good work. Surely we may depend upon them when they are offered that, and that only, as their reward. Surely when they find there is no alternative, no missions, no societies, no oratory, no advertisement, no money needed in the new method, they will not, like the unemployed, find out their mistake, and silently steal away.

Whether it will be the old, or whether a new set of philanthropists will require to grow up to put the new philanthropy in motion, we do not know ; but he must first teach himself, before he can become the mentor of the Poor. He must go among the Poor, not as a philanthropist but as a private individual, until he has taught himself to endure their sufferings firmly and

calmly. He has to teach himself what they can endure,
and what they cannot, before he can know what he has
to relieve, or what he has to help them to suffer. He
has to learn what *they* call hunger, and what they look
upon as only a passing privation, so that he may know
who to feed and who to leave alone. He must learn to
look unmoved upon habits foreign to his nature, and
tolerate sights that would be disgusting in his own
class. Until he can do so he will never know when he
is falling back into the weakness of seeking to improve
the Poor for his own sake, rather than for theirs.
Until he can see, and feel, and tolerate the lives of the
Poor as they themselves can do, he cannot know what
their disabilities are. Like the physician going through
his ward in the hospital, he must be able to endure the
sufferings of his patients without losing his sympathy,
or desire to help them. Nor should he stop there, but
cultivate a fortitude greater than that even of the Poor,
so as to have some reserve strength to fall back upon
on an emergency.

The Poor are in future to be treated as men, not as
women and children—as men with all the capacity
within themselves of taking up their own fortunes and
meeting their own responsibilities. They are to be
encouraged to do for themselves what the mission
has hitherto been doing for them. They are to be
invited to become part of the community, and to take
their share of helping forward its progress; their part
is to destroy misery, suffering, and distress in themselves individually, instead of as formerly merely
creating these things for others to attend to. Where
by reason of weakness they may be inclined to fail,
they are not to be relieved of the task, they are to be
strengthened and supported until they overcome it.

There is no such thing in any man's life as chronic distress; distress is incidental. All, then, that is required

is to teach the sufferer how to bear it, to help him to bear
it if necessary, but not to relieve him of it. That teaches
him nothing but weakness. The next time he will not
even endure so long before throwing his burden upon
you, and so on, until he will not even bear the apprehension of it ; from that also he must be relieved. The demand for a higher social condition is just the demand to
be relieved from the apprehension of distress. Under the
false teaching of their friends, the Poor just now believe
there is no duty incumbent upon them to contend with
distress. They make no effort to do so, and what is
worse, they make no effort to avoid causing it by their
own actions. There are many of their actions from
which they know distress must inevitably follow. But
what of that. They only look upon it as one of the
hard conditions of their lives, from which it is the duty
of the charitable to relieve them. The action is easily
avoidable ; but nobody has told them that they are
morally bound to avoid it ; or bear the punishment it
brings, without complaint or hope of relief. They
would do one or other if left alone ; but as the mission
only concerns itself with the distress, the Poor are not
inclined to endure where relief is offered, or give up a
habit that brings pleasure before the pain. The
pleasure they get ; the pain they avoid ; and so
Nature's law of " deterrent " is stultified.

There is no condition of life to which a workman might
aspire—artificial means, living wage, high organisation,
or what not—that is above the possibility or apprehension of distress. All that any of these states could
do, if attained, would be to show they were not high
enough for the purpose. On the other hand, there is
no condition so lowly, even to voluntary poverty, where
distress cannot be avoided, or endured with the
help and support of sympathetic friends. When a
person has to endure the consequences of his own

actions, it is natural in him to reduce their effects as
much as possible.   The practice of endurance makes a
man strong, physically and morally, courageous, self-
reliant, and fearless ; the practise of guiding our habits
so as to make endurance unnecessary makes a man
stronger, teaching self-control, self-denial, and independence.   All conduce to make a man the master of
his destiny.

If we can produce a man who, no matter how much
or how little he may earn, can so economise it that he
will always be able to supply him with such food and
clothing as he himself feels sufficient for his wants ; and
in the exceptional cases where he may fail, will feel it
incumbent upon himself to utilise his sufferings as a
stimulus to greater effort ; and to endure in silence, until
he has exhausted every means within his power to find
employment ; and only after total failure, feel justified
in seeking his fellow man's help.   If we can make, not
such a man, because there are plenty of them already,
but set in motion such a condition of life that will level
up all men to this standard of strength, because it is
only strength that is wanted, we believe we will have
done a good deal towards solving the question of social
poverty.   But what we aim at most, we believe we will
have helped the Poor themselves a step or two towards
their happiness.   Nor would it be the Poor only, who
would benefit individually by the change ; for if all the
classes above the Poor are levelled up to their standard
of strength, they will find in their own lives such an
infinitely better condition of things, that most of the
difficulties of their present life will vanish, solely from
the strength that is able to cope with them and fear
them not.

We say nothing whatever about religion, morality,
education, or temperance.   When the Poor have overcome the fear of want, they will have time to study these

N

things as their betters do. They are all easy to the
strong man; it is the weak who are always taking a
short cut through vice to gain their ends. But again,
on the other hand the strong man, although he
tolerates, is apt to despise authority, and the Poor in
their strength may throw these aside as obsolete
guides for an old and now impossible condition of life,
and take to cultivating virtues of their own, more in
accordance with their formed habits and the evolution
of them, into perfection. Further, in the case of the
strengthened Poor, these virtues, Religion, &c., would
have to be presented from a new standpoint. Just
now they are pressed upon them as infallible cures for
poverty. When the Poor have cured their own poverty
without the aid of these virtues they may still remain
as irreligious, immoral, ignorant, and intemperate as
many of their wealthy brethren of the present day who
never have had to fear want. In such a case these
virtues would have to be recommended to the Poor as
having some other attraction. But to ease the minds
of the timorous, we will add : Virtues are mostly
leading-strings for the weak, the strong man is in
himself virtue personified. All men are conscious that
the right path is the easiest, if one has the strength to
tread it. The strong man treads it from choice because
it is the easiest ; the short cuts of vice have no inducement for him, he sees so plainly that after all they are
the longest, most intricate, and toilsomest way round.

To change the confirmed habits of men is not a task
that can be accomplished in a year or two. There
is first the necessary preliminary of changing their
opinions, of convincing them that the change desired
will be beneficial to them. There is no man could
persuade the Poor, that the change we desire of them
will be for their good, to the extent of getting their
co-operation, but there is a voice the Poor are in the

habit of listening to that will bring conviction to them
where man would fail—the voice of Nature.   There
are three stages they must pass through ; the process
of disabusing their minds of their present convictions ;
their conversion by Nature ; and their co-operation
after conversion.

While this process is going on in the Poor, their
betters have also some duties to perform in connection
therewith.   The quickest way to persuade the Poor
that the opinions which they have been unfortunately
taught, and now firmly hold, namely that they are to
be allowed to create distress which it is the duty of
the better classes to relieve, is erroneous, is to with-
draw at once all eleemosynary aid, all extraneous
supports, no matter what the kind, and especially
missions of all kinds.   This of course will pain the
philanthropist much more than the Poor, because of his
greater weakness, but if he cannot do so much for those
he loves, how can he ask them to do anything for him ?
Among the Poor, those who will suffer most will be the
mission-parasites ; nor can we hope they will be inclined to try honest work again.   We expect they will
join the submerged tenth, and with their religious cant
make a great outcry that *they* are the deserving Poor,
the industrious idle, whom to feed and keep in idleness
is the first duty of the government, the first care of
the charitable.   But when no person heeds them,
none take note of them, with the astuteness of their
class they will see that, as they themselves would put
it, the game is up.   They will then be left with Dame
Nature, who will teach them that their enjoyment in
future, will be in proportion to their labour.

The thriftless, the improvident, and the self-indulgent,
who have got to believe that they have a right to spend
every penny upon themselves, that they earn, because
one mission is feeding, clothing, and holidaying their

children; while another is supplying their wives with
all their household wants; and a third revives and restores themselves on Sunday after their usual Saturday
debauch; these three types will take the change very
unkindly, will do all they can to try and evade having
to take the responsibilities of their families upon
themselves; and will loudly protest they are not able
to do so with the money that they earn. (Which is quite
true, as long as they spend it in their customary
manner.) But when they find they are talking to
closed ears, or when a person comes forward and
offers to take their wages and feed and clothe their
family with it, they too will find Dame Nature waiting
to teach them the economy of life.

There is another type, though on rather a different
footing, that has something to unlearn; the willing-to-
work-but-can't-find-it unemployed. This person has
been unfortunately taught that, should he happen to
be dismissed, from dulness of trade or other cause, he
is not required to look for work again, unless in his
own immediate neighbourhood; nor to accept of it even
then, unless it be the same work as he is accustomed
to, at the highest current rate of wages, with the
shortest hours, and all other superior conditions of his
trade; and that if these cannot be found (and it is not
likely they are to be found in a neighbourhood where
men are being paid off from slackness of trade), he has
a just claim upon the government to find them for him.
Before this person can be disillusionised, the better
classes must be well on their way in the accumulation of strength. They must have cultivated it
sufficiently that we can have a Parliament of strong
men, not the Government only, but the whole Parliament, so strong that they will fear no party sufficiently,
to flatter them; strong enough for the fever of
philanthropy for philanthropy's sake to have subsided

in them ; for their brains to be cool and firm, and see
only the good of any class in its bearings upon the
good of all ; strong enough to care so little for
place, as to be unshaken by its temptations ; strong
enough to deprecate legislation, and teach in its place
mutual concession and arrangement. Such a Government would tell the industrious idle (of the present
conception) that the term "unemployed" means a
person, who when he finds himself out of employment,
seeks for work in every quarter of the country where it
is likely to be found, offers to take any kind of work
he is capable of, and at whatever remuneration that is
tendered, until the depression in his own particular
trade is past. That every person claiming the assistance of Government must make a declaration that they
have done all this and still failed, otherwise they are
classed with the voluntary idle. The Government,
while declaring that it is not within its province to
take notice of the occupation or profession of any
individual, may on economic grounds, offer the unemployed work on terms sufficiently below the ordinary
rate to make what to it is unnecessary and un-
desirable employment, profitable.

This class, however, are not exactly of the distressful
Poor ; they are only bothered with the over-develop-
ment of the Economy of Effort in them. They desire
that the Government should do that for them which they
are best able to do for themselves, and when the
Government declines the duty, there will be few of this
willing-to-work-but-can't-find-it class. But there will
always be some, and on their behalf, and on the behalf
of others, this strong Government has a further duty to
perform, and that is, to curb the power of the trade
societies as regards their right to make rules that there
shall only be one standard wage in every trade. There
is no reason why these societies should declare the

industrial world to be the monopoly of the young and vigorous only ; and that is the actual result of such a law. Further, it is making the period in a man's life of capacity for labour shorter and shorter, and the selection of men more limited every year. Thus it is increasing the number of men who, with still plenty of work in them, but not just enough for the high pressure an employer requires for the high wages demanded of him, are compelled to remain idle, and the employer and unemployed are not allowed to make any compromise. And, further, the high pressure of work, high wages, and a corresponding high life, make premature old men of the workmen, and have been the prolific cause of the increase of old age pauperism, and the demand for old age pensions at fifty-five years of age.

Defective energy is almost always accompanied with a proportionate lowness of desire, and the weak are quite willing to take less for their work than their more vigorous brethren, making their smaller wage do all for them that the greater wage does for the other. And with waning strength it is the same. It is a question if the failing of strength is not first exhibited in the failing of desire ; and that that period in our lives when the philosophers tell us that Reason is beginning to assume its sway over Passion, is nothing more than that the vigour that incited the passion is diminishing ; and with a less urgent passion to blind us, Reason can see more clearly the issue of our actions.

It was Legree the slave-driver who believed that the most economical way of dealing with his slaves was to work them at high pressure for the few years they could stand it, and then purchase fresh ones. There are also some coach and cab proprietors in large towns who believe the same about horses. They say that the period of usefulness of hackneys in large towns is short, and it is most profitable to take it out of them as soon as possible, then get rid of them, and get new ones. There are others who believe in the opposite plan, that if man or animal is never worked in a day more than the night's rest can amply restore, there is work in both up to almost their last days.

In their arguments for Government protection from idleness, the leaders of the workmen have asserted the claim that men who are willing to work should have work. Let the Government take them at their word, so far as to see these leaders do not put obstruction in the way themselves. Give every man the right to work at whatever wages is mutually agreed upon between himself and his employer. The workman does not work for his society, but for the man who pays him his wages. It is a private contract between them with which no one should have a right to interfere. The differentiation of wages can quite easily co-exist with a standard rate for the able-bodied full-timer, and that standard would be the guide for the differentiation; thus protecting the weak from imposition, if such were attempted.

When there is payment by capacity, then the under-energised would find permanent work, as well as the vigorous. The waning strength would be content to work at a lower rate, in preference to being idle. Even old age would not be refused whatever it could do, for whatever it could get, and its independence would not be assailed. A great number of the submerged tenth would be absorbed on terms suitable to their capacity. But the great advantage would be that the pressure of toil would instantly be lowered to a safe and healthy state. Even the vigour of manhood would prefer a steadier, evener condition of life, with a view to a longer period of preserved strength. There would be no Eight hours question requiring to be settled. Men would not be so exhausted with their labour as to look with favour upon eight hours compulsory rest every day, without adequate means to enjoy them. Each trade or work would settle its own hours on the principle of the amount of toil required in its exercise. Workmen would carry their energies long past the present presumed age of incapacity—fifty-five. At sixty and sixty-five they would be independent ; and the old age pension question would settle itself by most of them being able to die in harness. The others could easily be dealt with. Finally, there would be a more vigorous, less toil-weary race of workmen, who would transmit their vigour to their children, and each succeeding generation would grow in that strength which is the root of all happiness, and the solvent of all difficulties.

So much for the first, or unlearning stage. Let us now consider the second, or convincing stage.

CHAPTER XII

Nature as an educator—The duties of the new philanthropist
Nature's law of Deterrents—Their educative force—Weakness will endure certain deterrents for the indulgence in
certain habits—The moral teaching of fisticuffs.

IT is a favourite sentiment with the pious, that "as
gold is refined by fire, so the heart must be tried (or
purified) by pain." It is an extraordinary thing that
they never tried this sentiment upon the Poor! It
could have been done so easily. The Poor had plenty
of pain ; but instead of waiting its chastening effects,
the whole effort of the philanthropist was to relieve
them of their distress, and then attempt to chasten
their hearts by argument. Perhaps they thought the
Poor were not fit subjects for the practice of such a
beautiful sentiment. If so, it is the only sentiment we
know, that they have not practised upon the Poor.
Perhaps they thought that the lesson of pain could
only appeal to those who knew its meaning—that,
what is the fact, one has first to be pious before pain
will make him any more so ; and conversely, the
irreligious before pain are left irreligious still by its

experience. The beautiful and pious sentiment is only a poetic attempt at expressing the common pheno- menon that pain is weakness, and in our weakness we seek for aid where we believe we will find it—the pious to their religion ; the Poor to the mission ; and the weak to the strong. But the persons who have no recourse but to endure it, do so in the different phases of their strength—the strong, silently ; the middle strength that fears it may overwhelm him, like the stag at bay, with anger and fury ; and the weak, querulously or noisily.

Nature's true lesson of pain, however, is pithily summed up in the proverb—" A burnt bairn dreads the fire." Instead of pain being a purifier, or the hand- maid of religion or anything else, it is simply a deter- rent. That is Nature's use for it, and for that she created it. In our original state (and to a large extent yet) any violation of her laws brought pain. Her teaching is wholly virtuous ; every action that she dictates is to bring happiness ; but every attempt to alter or avoid her laws is met with the deterrent pain. Man who has spent his time in trying to improve upon Nature has got no farther yet. The world is still governed by the dread of pain. There are some religions profess to teach by love, but in the matter of education, love is only indulgence, or the process of making my will more agreeable to you than your own, a system that may suit the nursery, but would bankrupt any institution or Government in a week.

In our original state the nature within us formulated the body's demands ; not only in the broad principles of hunger, thirst, and rest which we still retain, but was perfect and comprehensive over the whole world of our knowledge, choosing the exact fruit, or root, or blade of grass, as the case might be. So far, with infallible machinery that governed our actions to the smallest detail, we could not have erred ; and if we

could not have erred we should have required no inhibitive faculty, and no deterrent. But there was also
in us a law called the Economy of Effort, and that law
was a continual temptation to ignore Nature's demands
because of the trouble they would cost, and also, when
once stirred to action, was inclined to oversupply itself
to avoid future trouble ; therefore, to counteract such a
possibility, Nature added pain as a penalty for the
breach of any of its laws.

The ethics of Nature are pleasure unaccompanied
with pain, or pleasure accompanied with pain. There
must always be pleasure in our free actions, because
we are following our destiny of seeking our happiness.
But the right way is unaccompanied by pain or evil
result, and the wrong way is accompanied by a deterrent as a cause for remembrance and regret. It is by
this primitive code we leave the Poor in Nature's hands
to be educated.

In doing so we know we are open to the charge of
dealing in heroic treatment, or, from another point
of view, may be called harsh, cruel, and hard-hearted.
We are quite aware, as we write this, that it is as
impossible for the philanthropical classes in their
present weak condition, to permit the Poor to endure
the natural consequences of their own actions, as for a
young mother to keep from cuddling her baby, although
the doctor may have warned her, she does so at great
risk to its existence. It is not the child that requires
the cuddling, but the mother. In like manner, it would
not be what the Poor would suffer, but what the
philanthropists would. But until they allow the Poor
to learn to avoid suffering in themselves, suffering
will continue to increase, instead of diminishing.

All what we call the softer or humanising virtues are
the product of weakness, and minister to and create
further weakness. They are, in their effect upon man

and his future happiness, but gilded vices. That Mercy that descends like the dew from heaven, is our inability to contemplate, let alone enforce, the punishments we have decreed for certain offences. It is no uncommon thing for that Anger which is so characteristic of weakness, to have decreed a more vigorous punishment than a calmer state of mind can look upon as just, and so one weakness is set to counteract another—the weakness of mercy recoiling from the weakness of anger : thus we are afraid to put in force our own decrees. In other cases, we make penalties, only looking at them as deterrents, and when they fail as such, we are incapable of contemplating them as punishments. But the common springs of Mercy are our degeneracy. Punishments that come down to us from a stronger age, when deterrents had to be measured by our powers of pain endurance, are now declared inhuman, barbarous, and brutal. Thus we flatter our weakness, and make a virtue of our inability to contemplate, let alone endure, pain. Yet by such action we do not reduce the causes of pain—we increase them, and increase our fear of it. Our fear of it, we call tenderness of heart, and refined sensibility. We cultivate it in ourselves and encourage it in others ; and the fear of pain is the parent of vice.

We all know that the Perpetual Petitioners for the Remission of all Punishments are the weakest, most invertebrate, and hysterical of the community. They are composed of women and clergymen, and they believe their folly is dictated by the highest sentiments the heart is capable of. Whether it is the murderer or the murderess, the thief in good society, or only the person who may have a child born during the period of incarceration, it is all the same to them. They cannot endure the contemplation of suffering, and because they cannot, the laws of the land are to be set aside ; but

rouse the same people's anger and there is no punishment, however severe, they cannot revel in. Read the
reports of the assizes ; there is no one so bad that he
cannot get a clergyman to give him a good character,
even if the crime has been carefully premeditated or
long indulged in. When there is no defence, lawyers
are hired to tell a pathetic story. New defences spring
up every day ; "contributory negligence," when a man
trusts his servant to go to the bank for him, and does
not immediately take measures to see that he has gone
and performed the business required of him ; "undue
temptation" when a man's wages are not in proportion
to the money he handles ; "irresponsibility for his
actions," when a man, not having the courage to fight
his enemy sober, gets drunk for the purpose, and
perhaps kills him.

These, and even more trivial appeals for mercy,
would not be so continuously offered if they had no
effect ; but we know they have an effect, and see that
some judges welcome them as an excuse for miti-
gation. We only mention this, to show that there is
throughout the length and breadth of the land, a nervous
desire to avoid the natural consequences of our actions,
if they are painful.

The tender-hearted need not fear we are going to
desert the Poor however. There will always be plenty
of silent watchers to see that none are over-burdened ;
plenty to encourage them. But it is necessary that as
far as the Poor are concerned, they will remain to them
unknown and unseen. We are informed that the
troops that are sent to the West Indies become in two
or three years quite enervated. The climate is too
equable ; it is a perpetual summer and "always afternoon," and in it the troops become weak and exhausted.
They have to be sent to the rigorous winters of Canada
to brace them up, and restore their relaxed energies.

Just such a process have the Poor to go through. Out from the mephitic, heated atmosphere of contending charities, the Poor are to be braced and strengthened by independence. It will be a cold, a vigorous, and a frosty atmosphere, but it is necessary so to be, to call into play their relaxed energies. The person who hitherto spent all that he earned on wage-day, will have six days' hunger to contend with. He will not like it, and soon he will refuse to suffer. He may try to do with food on alternate days, which will only make the hunger of the off-days more keen. By and by, he will learn to distribute his money over the whole week. When he does so he will have learned much ; he will have learned self-restraint, the first step to all reform ; he will have learned the self-denial that leads to thrift, whether he desires to pursue it to that extent or not. Having learned to refuse his desires while he has the money to gratify them, because the money is required for other purposes in the course of the week, he can also refuse his desires while in possession of the means of gratifying them, for any other purpose that may appeal to his self-interest. And so by a course of treatment of this nature, not for a few years only, or any time so short that the Poor would refuse to learn their lesson, but for all time, the wage-earner would avoid giving himself any suffering to bear that could be avoided, either by the imitation of a higher life than he can comfortably maintain, or by indulgence one day at the expense of another. To have learned to expend their earnings as judiciously as they could, and to have made every personal effort to earn enough for their wants, is all we can ask of any class or person.

There will ever be a time when desire will overcome habit and resolution, and suffering must follow ; but the weakness that fell before desire will be ashamed to

expose its sufferings ; and resolution will be called up
to help the unfortunate to endure in silence until the
incident is past. Nor will such a lesson be wholly lost.
There are all the unforeseen incidents of life that cannot
be provided against. These are divided into two
classes : the sudden loss of income, and exceptional
circumstances that call for extra expenditure. These
are met by the other classes, especially the lower
middle classes, with fortitude and resolution, and
sometimes secrecy ; and the Poor having learned to
meet their own sufferings with courage, will also
struggle with those that are thrust upon them. Nor is
the comparison between the lower middle classes and
the Poor in the face of unforeseen calamity an unfair
one to the latter. It is thought that the Poor, living as
they do from hand to mouth, are less protected against
misfortune than any other class. But this is not the
case. We might even say, that for true heroic endurance in the face of sudden distress, the lower middle
classes take the palm. All the lower middle classes
live at a higher rate than their means warrant. It is
they who have the true struggle to make ends meet.
This is owing to the social rivalries of the women.
Successful rivalry is the one aim and object of their
lives. From that cause alone they are the most moral
of the classes, as they have to practise every self-denying
virtue. But from that cause also they are least
protected against emergency. Yet they have to assume
the virtue which they are far from possessing, and so
they bear their burdens not only with courage, but with
the smiling face of plenty.

The Poor have many means of fortifying each other
to bear their misfortunes. They have nothing else.
They have no money to purchase relief ; but they have a
ready sympathy, and willing hands to help to make misfortune endurable. This is the charity of the Poor, true

charity, and all have heard how much the Poor do for one another.

Sudden forms of misfortune the Poor have to suffer at present, because they are not of a kind that the missions can reach until the acute stage is past. But they bear them sullenly, unwillingly, and with a grudge against society, sometimes, as being the cause of them ; but whether or no, from the confirmed conviction that they should be protected from all suffering, like so many children. When they have learned to take up the burden of their own lives, they will also see that they must, like all the other classes, include its never absent chapter of accidents ; and with free trade in employment, and the final refuge in Government work, misfortunes must be easily recoverable.

As there are forms of voluntary poverty, so also there are forms of voluntary distress, and although the Poor have their share of it, they have no monopoly. It may seem strange, that with every faculty within us made to detect and recoil from pain, we yet voluntarily invite it. Not the Poor alone, not any class or nation, but the whole world according to their several degrees of strength, the strong man least and the weak one most ; all are in the habit of knowingly inflicting upon them-selves avoidable pain. The drunkard is only a glaring type of an universal habit—the willingness to endure the penalties of our actions, for the pleasure of them. Women are the grossest example of this habit ; they endure physical pain, some almost constantly, for sake of their fashions ; they cultivate bodily ailments that produce sickness and accelerate death, by habits they are prone to, and refuse to give up. How few have reached middle life that have not continued the habit, or resumed it, that their physician has warned them to give up ! What man has died whose friends do not know the habit that helped to carry him off?

Nor is the habit confined to vicious or immoral action ; it is as common and as hurtful in actions that are approved of by religion and society.

Nature made no protection against this violation of her laws. All things she gave life to, she endowed with sufficient strength to hold their place in the cosmogony of the world, and as the greater the strength we possess the less strong our desires, so her deterrents were made for the strong and not for the weak. Thus the weakness in us sets her punishments at defiance in pleasures that have become necessary to us.

The test of pleasure is the sense of strength it imparts. As pain is weakness, so pleasure is strength, and the more strength we possess in ourselves the less we seek from outside sources. Conversely, the weaker we are the more dependent on extraneous aids we become. Habit, again, destroys the native strength in us, that is the equivalent of what it supplies, until we are forced to depend entirely on it for strength, instead of ourselves.

Drinking is the most pleasurable of all habits, and that is the reason it is most common—universal, unless where forbidden by religion. It gives strength to the consumer more quickly, more fully, and with the least trouble of any other pleasure in the world. The rapidity with which it stimulates, counteracting depression, weariness, and weakness, makes it invaluable to those who have learned to rely upon it. Its deterrent is great, and its after-suffering sometimes awful, yet they are not a sufficient counter-check to the habit, and all the additional punishments man has added, and threatened to add, have been of no avail. Because of the very fulness of strength it imparts, it plays havoc in proportion with the natural strength it supplants, and its votaries are quickly reduced to a weakness that makes them wholly dependent upon it for any pleasure

or strength they can have. In such cases it is not a
matter of self-denial, or strength to resist the temptation. In obedience to the law of destiny whereby they
must seek their happiness, those who have set their
happiness in this habit will fight for it with all their
strength and knowledge. Not till we cultivate strength
within the human frame up to the point where stimulation
is unnecessary, will the drinking habit become unde-
sirable. Not until we have recovered sufficient strength
to have restored Nature's punishments to their true
position of deterrents, will the whole fabric of indulgence
in vicious habits disappear.

Over the persons who have made drink a necessity
of their lives, Natural law can have no influence, neither
hitherto have the additional punishments which the
laws of the country sometimes inflict. On the other
hand, to relieve them of the consequences of their own
acts, is only to encourage them. Therefore the first
thing the new philanthropist has to learn is to distinguish between voluntary and involuntary distress
among the Poor, as he has also to learn to distinguish
between voluntary and involuntary poverty. It is not
necessary to tell the philanthropist how this information
can be acquired. The policemen on the beat know
these men at a glance ; the publicans know them ; the
keepers of the lodging- and doss-houses know them ;
and the honest Poor who live among them know them.
It is not that the philanthropist should go to any of
these authorities to acquire the information that we
mention them, although the philanthropist may consult
any of them on an emergency, but that he should learn
his own lesson as they have learned theirs, by experience.

We will now give the new philanthropist a sketch of
his duties. When you go amongst the Poor take next
to no money with you. No matter in what guise you

go you will be "spotted"; and from previous education every one of the undeserving Poor will suspect you to be upon a philanthropic mission, with money to disburse. You will be told by every one whom you approach the most pitiful stories of hardship and poverty imaginable, and if you do not offer money, it will be asked of you. If you remain adamant to these appeals then they will conclude you suspect their sincerity, and on your next visit they will have a "living picture" of poverty arranged for you, and having told their well-concocted story, will insist that you can prove the truth of it by coming with them to see. If you are once weak enough to give them money, you had best leave that district and never return to it. Your usefulness will be gone ; you will never be allowed to recover yourself ; you will never be believed in your assertion that you are going to discontinue the habit ; but the distress in that neighbourhood will grow apace and flourish for your benefit.

When you have thoroughly persuaded all and sundry with whom you come in contact, that you are not going to deal in money on any account, then the pests will leave you ; indeed you will be severely left alone by every person—the honest Poor not desiring money of you, and the dishonest having been refused it. You will then be in a first-class position to study the Poor without molestation. Your next move is to map out the limits of your operations, making them small rather than large, and you will familiarise yourself with your locality by strolling slowly through it while you are studying the population. By this process you will also become recognised by its inhabitants, and when you begin your mission work you will find this of great advantage. If you see a broil, neither run into it nor run away from it. In the first case you do not know enough of its origin to be a judge ; and in the second

case you are not fit to do the Poor any good, if you are
not strong enough to look upon their quarrels as calmly
and unflinchingly as they look upon them themselves.
And further, unless in a case of gross unfairness, make
a habit of non-interference. If you interfere between
men quarrelling you will create a prejudice against
yourself, not only by the combatants, but by the on-
lookers, which you will find, by their withdrawing their
sympathy from you, will militate against your work.
When you have become used to the Poor you will find
that fisticuffs, instead of being brutal and degrading, is
the most healthful and moral way of settling their
disputes. Why we should encourage in our boys at
school what we condemn in grown-up men seems
strange, but is accounted for by the argument of our
own weakness. We are stronger than our youths ; we
can endure their little fights because we believe they
cannot hurt each other much ; but when they become
men and can deal each other blows at which we
shudder, then fighting is brutal and degrading. We do
not prohibit it because we can no longer bear it, which
is the true and only reason we have against it. Pages
have been written about the manliness, courage, and
moral healthiness that school-fighting teaches boys.
How can all these virtues pass from it when it is practised by old boys? When do the virtues die out of this
habit, and the vices grow into it? Is there any other
habit of life that has this chameleon-like quality of
changing its merits with age? And if it does not
change, then it must always be vicious, and we should
not allow our boys to practise it ; or it must be always
virtuous, no matter the age of the belligerents.

At the school age boys are still much in the hands of
Nature ; their inhibitive and reflected faculties are
almost dormant ; their energy is great, and urgent to
action ; and is only partially restrained by their imper-

fect knowledge of conventional right and wrong. All
these things combine to retain in them their naturally
high individuality. Their actions are quick to follow
their desires, and are mostly selfish. This is quite
harmless when they are alone ; they are then subject to
Nature's deterrents. But when civilisation compels
them to live with a great many other boys, they have
to learn the code by which boys live together.
No teaching in the world would ever be effective,
because their actions are too rapid for reflection. Their
lesson might be impressed upon them every day ; in an
hour they would break it before they knew, and then for
the rest of the day they would be miserable and unhappy.
But the boys know a far better way, and copying the
Nature that teaches them through pain, they erect
combat as a deterrent. Without that, the strong would
be bullies and tyrants, the weak, sneaks, liars, and
thieves. Every boy in a school where fighting is
allowed, knows that if he says or does anything to the
hurt of one of his schoolmates, he must do so at the
risk of what punishment the injured one can inflict upon
him ; and every boy knows he must live himself so
morally, according to school morals, that he must be
prepared to defend his reputation against every insinu-
ation. Thus boys are taught to be truthful ; as they
dare not risk a false charge ; they are taught to be
courageous, and just : just, to apologise if they have
made a false statement ; courageous, to defend the truth
when they have proclaimed it. If we had a kind of
machinery that would have a similar effect through life
upon both men and women ; one that compelled us to be
truthful, just, and brave to our neighbours, while at the
same time it constrained us to live a life of honour and
honesty that we must be prepared at any moment to defend ; no matter how harsh it might seem, the world would
rise and call it blessed, instead of brutal and degrading.

If we want to know the value of fisticuffs as a moral agent we have only to compare a boys' school with a girls' school. We have no wish to be severe upon the girls—the fault does not lie with them, but with their system of education—but we know that the recognised untruthfulness, unfairness, and cruelty the sex practises upon its own members is learned as early as, and sometimes earlier than, the school age ; when girls find there is no physical punishment to act as a deterrent in their conduct towards each other, they find no natural consequences flowing from their actions to guide and restrain them.

The Poor in many respects are just like schoolboys. They have never learned to express themselves by argument. The expression of their thoughts and intentions during their working hours is by action, and the habit is confirmed in them. When they quarrel, they have no language but the personal and offensive kind that only aggravates the matter. They have not been educated to a brain repression that can supplant instantaneous revenge with a permanent dislike and desire for reprisals. A few blows are interchanged (both parties are sufficiently strong to ignore the physical pain), and all is over. The combatants may be separated by friends, or may become immediately afterwards drinking cronies. The cause of the row is past and gone ; neither bears resentment, neither carries away any evil intention against his neighbour.

The Poor could not live as they do, upon the street, everybody being hail-fellow-well-met with everybody else, unless they had a rough-and-ready method of settling their disputes, and one that acts as a wholesome deterrent against disputes arising. They cannot get away from each other by shutting themselves up in their houses as the classes do, and without that essential, the rest of the plan would only produce a

hell-on-earth among them. When the better classes
quarrel they have the courage to slander, but not to
fight. They nurse their resentment for a lifetime ; ever
vigilant to do their enemy every harm they can. They
leave their feuds to their children as solemn obligations
to the dead. They divide their social world, making
enemies of all who show any sympathy with their
opponent. They widen and widen the area of the
feud until whole clans are involved in it. They pride
themselves on the steadfastness and durability of their
hate. They ruin the lives of children as yet unborn,
as in *Romeo and Juliet*. And all this from no other
cause of quarrel than a rash or heedless word, or
biting their thumbs at each other.

If the Poor in a single street made every quarrel a
vendetta, sought partisans, and continued the feud
every night, would it be a less brutal and degrading
spectacle than their present method of settling it at
once, and washing away all recollection of it afterwards
in a glass of beer ?

These sudden quarrels of the Poor are never long,
because of the fear of the police, and they are generally
as harmless as a French duel. But sometimes there
are accidents. Sometimes a man gets killed, or his
skull fractured by falling on the kerbstone, or an arm
or a leg gets broken in the fray. These results are all
pure accidents ; but when they get into the papers
there is a great outcry about them. But when we take
the trouble to average them, we find that there is not
recorded a serious accident from fighting more than
about once a week ; and there must be among the
industrial centres of the country thousands of quarrels
every night. During the hunting season there were
far more accidents—fatal and maiming—caused by
hunting. During the boating season there is an
enormously higher death-rate from drowning than

quarrelling. The proportion of serious hurt from fighting is something next to deaths from railway travelling—something microscopical to the million carried.

When, therefore, you see a quarrel among the Poor, do not interfere unless there is gross injustice being done ; and should such be the case there will be plenty of others to interfere more effectively than you. But when the combat is over, see to the defeated. No matter how ugly his wounds may look (if he has got any), do not judge them by their appearance, but as the sufferer judges them ; he may be stronger than you. Make light of them if he makes light of them. Should he complain of them, then help him to a surgery to have them attended to. But do not let him get faint-hearted under them. Encourage him to endure, although you do all in your power to heal his wounds. When our little toddling child falls, we pick him up, and see to the wound. When we have satisfied ourselves it is but trifling, we minimise it to him to hush his crying ; we make light of it, to teach him to endure, to be manly and courageous, and not cry at every hurt. Why we do not do so with our fellow-man is because we cannot endure his hurt ourselves. But if we could, and could teach him to do so also, we should raise the point of endurance higher in us all, and to do so is not only to conquer so much distress, but to acquire so much solid virtue—virtue that will not be shown only in physical fortitude, but in every action of our lives, and in every thought that governs our actions. It is our sense of strength that makes us think aright, as it is our weakness that suggests easier courses.

Should you see a drunkard staggering along the street, follow him until you see if he can navigate himself along without molestation. If he can do so, you have nothing further to do with him ; if he is incapable, keep him from being abused until you find a policeman to take care of him. We do not advise this from any lack of sympathy, but from experience we find the station is the safest place for an incapable. There are no rest-houses or shelters for inebriates, but the police station-houses. There, they are in safety, and out of harm's way. There, they have better conditions than at home, as a rule : they have quietude and rest, general supervision, and, if neces-sary, medical attendance. We are informed that it is a general rule with the police, that if the inebriates are unfamiliar to the authorities, and have not been disorderly, they are generally dismissed in the morning without a charge being made against them. If such is the case—and we know it to be the rule in some towns—then you are doing an " incapable " no harm, but good, in giving him into the care of the police. But if the person should happen to be one of those volun-tary sufferers for drink's sake, then you have the advantage of the police's knowledge as well as your own.

CHAPTER XIII

The New Philanthropist as Doctor and Nurse—A continuation of his duties.

WHEN you feel strong enough to take up your work, your first duty is to cultivate the acquaintance of all and sundry on your beat—the street-corner men, the loafers, the police and shopkeepers ; the drunkards, thieves, and harlots. Not by specially seeking them out, but by having a cheery word for everybody you meet. You must always be ready to enter into conversation with them on a footing of perfect equality and friendship, because it is through them you will know where the true distress is. You must put aside all your prejudices, and bury for the time being all your class morality ; you must put on your armour of strength, and say "I will do no wrong." And unless you feel you can talk to anybody and everybody without being defiled, you are not yet strong enough ; and unless you feel you can resist what you hold to be wrong, even when desirous for sympathy's sake, you are not yet strong enough. And further, until you can suppress the desire to advocate your own morality,

as a prophylacteric against the strange doctrines you
will hear, you are not yet strong enough. You must
not talk morality to the Poor, or they will at once
suspect the cloven hoof of the mission, and all
sympathy between you will be gone. But you will get
plenty of opportunities without seeking them. They
will appeal to you readily as to the right or wrong of
their actions. Then you can tell them what you would
do, and what you would not do; but you must not
condemn. You will find no one will press you to do
anything you say you cannot do for conscience sake;
but on the other hand, you are not to expect that your
refusal should so influence them that they also will
forego the action, whatever it might be. That will
often happen, but not always. More commonly they
will not offend you by doing it in your presence. Do
not deduce from that that they are not guilty of it in
your absence, and finding such to be the case get
angry.

When you have gained their confidence, and when
they have come to know you, then they will tell you
of the true cases of distress in your neighbourhood,
and as long as you do not give them any money you
may rely upon the cases they point out to you being
genuine; and further, as long as you show you are
prepared to give time and trouble to help them to bear
their burdens, their sympathies will be with you, and
they will be very jealous of who requires your services,
to see that you are not imposed upon. When you
break this rule, there will be a scramble among them
who will get your ear first, to get your largesse.

If you are informed of a workman being out of work,
interest yourself in him. Find out what his occupation
is, and where he worked last. Inquire among your
friends where such kind of work is likely to be had,
but do not give him money to live upon in the mean-

time ; give him encouragement and work—work in finding out where work is to be had. See him every day until he is successful, and when you find he is coming near extreme poverty, ask an employer to give him work for a fortnight, and you will pay the employer what difference he will require as between what the man is worth and the standard rate of wages : a fortnight or a month according to your means, but never more than a month at a time. When your object becomes known, many employers will oblige you without asking any money from you, if you do not abuse their kindness by sending too many idle men to them. The workman is not to know of your arrangement, neither are the workmen in the employers' service, When you have found work for your unemployed, you do not tell him so, but give him the address as a likely place to find work, and get him to promise to call. Then you will know whether he is desirous of work or not. If he calls he will get employment, and if you still find him idle, he has evidently not applied. The reason why we limit his employment at your expense to a fortnight, is because two or three weeks' wages will start him again to look for work on his own account, and the cost to you will be no more than if you had given him money, even a shilling a day when you first found him unemployed. Remember that, in dealing with a wage-earner, there are always two motives working in him, that make him more reluctant to search for work than an employee of the other classes. The change from labour to leisure is more grateful to him than to the warehouseman or clerk. The social stigma of idleness in their case, soon to be seen in the reduced economy of the household, does not affect him ; and so the excitement that counteracts his economy of effort is wanting ; and from his habit of looking to be paid for everything he does, he weighs the probability of success of any and every exertion he is asked to make, with a strong prejudice against it, a prejudice he makes no effort to overcome, unless he is almost assured it will be successful. Against this inertia the workman must always be stimulated. There are many we have known, capable of retaining their work when it has been found for them, but unable to overcome their disinclination to look for fresh work when out of a job. The charity of a shilling a night to some of these to get them a supper and breakfast, to fit them to look for work the next day, has often made them contented to remain idle if their clothes were good, and their bed sure ; and the slightest expression upon your part to look for work for a man will instantaneously make him drop all effort on his own account, in addition to holding you responsible, as it were, for his continued idleness if you fail. When you have got a workman employment in the manner we have suggested, the employer will be the best man to tell you if he be worthy of further solicitude. If he be a good and willing workman, the employer may find room for him on his permanent staff ; but if that is impossible, you will have confidence in recommending him to some other employer.

In regard to your use of money that is only employed in cases, not only of great necessity, but when all other plans fail. Resist the temptation to escape from their suffering by giving them money to relieve it. When you have to give them money it must always be in conjunction with your services to see them through their trouble, not instead of doing so. All the money you will require to use will be very little. Remember always, you are acting towards them as one of themselves, ready with your services and better knowledge to help them through their troubles. They never have, themselves, more than a shilling or so, and so you are

not required to have any more either. Always expend
the money yourself, that is, purchase for them the things
they require, things they absolutely cannot do without,
and that there is no other way of getting. It is not
from want of confidence in the Poor we advise this.
The mission-philanthropist could not trust the Poor
with money because it generally went in drink. This
was because he could not tell genuine from fraudulent
distress, and most cases were fraudulent because the
philanthropist could not himself endure distress ; and so,
like a coward in face of it, or a harrowing tale of it, he
paid the money and ran away. Your reasons are
different. Your cases are genuine, and your confidence
firm, and, further, you are not afraid of suffering ; but
there is this : your idea of the purchasing power of
money, and that of the Poor is different. In your
economy, a half a crown does not go far ; but with the
Poor a shilling will go further. The rich philanthropist
who gives money to the Poor does so according to his
own valuation of money, not theirs. A shilling is thrown
to one, where a few coppers were all that was required ;
half a crown where a shilling would suffice, and so on.
Then the desire for money springs up anew. When the
Poor have satisfied their legitimate demands from money
thus received, the overplus is very agreeable spending ;
so agreeable that it becomes their paramount desire, to
which all things must serve ; and their future distresses
come thick and fast, to be dressed up with an eye to
securing the greatest surplus for future enjoyment.

It is so difficult, you may never be able to know what
is the purchasing value of money to the Poor, and for
that reason you must buy yourself the things they stand
in need of.

All cases that are of greater magnitude than can be
met by temporary relief of the slightest kind, are not
for temporary assistance, but to be dealt with perma-

nently by the proper parties. Temporary relief not
only does no good, but because it is pleasant, creates a
reluctance on the part of the Poor to face a permanent
settlement of their difficulties. A woman who may be
suddenly left destitute, either by the death or desertion
of her husband, and who is unable to work for her
family, cannot be kept for life on personal charity.
Whether a settlement of her case is made by an allowance being granted by her relatives, or she has to go to
the workhouse, the matter should be gone into and
settled at once. The woman is in no wise benefited by
temporary aliment ; on the contrary, as charity is likely
to be more generous to her than her permanent settlement, she will be, because of it, more reluctant to enter
the latter, and discontented when she does. It is therefore your duty in this and all other cases of distress not
to think of temporary relief, but to set in action at once
the permanent cure for them. This is the keynote of
your whole position. Their sufferings will absorb them
to the exclusion almost of the power of action ; even if
they knew the right course to follow, their weakness
under distress would always suggest to them temporary
and immediate relief, without consideration of after
effect or permanent good. It is your place to supply to
them the strength their sufferings have robbed them of.
What is that in social life but active sympathy ? But
your sympathy must not only be active, it must be
experienced, full of knowledge and power, practised in
ready resources against emergencies, and acquainted
with all the permanent methods of relief that legally
exist. You are the person who comes to them fresh and
strong, to give their case your clear, unafflicted brain,
to give them your well-stored energy, to put to their use
your knowledge of their case and its cure, and to see
the latter entered upon and pursued to the end. You
are, in fact, to be both their physician and nurse, but

more their nurse. The doctor sometimes himself falls sick, and becomes so weak mentally and physically, that although he knows what his case requires he has not the strength to follow his own prescription. It is the nurse that supplies the strength, that does such work for him as he could not do for himself, that raises him in her arms, and helps him to do things he otherwise were unequal to. With all his knowledge, he would be in danger of death without the strength the nurse supplies him with. This is the true case with the Poor and the friends who would help them; it is only strength they want. Every man and woman knows how they would contend with their misfortunes if they had but the strength; but the plans they can all solve, and the difficulties they can overcome, while these difficulties are at a distance, are no longer possible to them when a difficulty is upon them. They had forgotten, that with the distress upon them, they would be weakened so by it that they would not have the strength to pursue their plan. They generally find they are so prostrated by their suffering, as to be incapable of thinking of plans of any kind, and shudder even at the contemplation of any part in one they may be required to perform. But when a friend restores to them that which they have lost—the cool brain to consider their case, as they did when it was afar off, and the energy and vigour of body to carry it out; to do for the sufferers what they are no longer able to do for themselves, to help them to do as much for themselves as they can—then their energy quickly comes back; their minds are lifted from their troubles, to become interested in the success of their efforts, and their difficulties soon vanish.

Thus, while it is your duty to qualify yourself, as far as you can, to be a physician of the Poor; to know where work may be found when it is wanted, and to learn how best to settle the troubles that you are likely to meet

with during your work, still you will find the most
effective part of your services will be in the character of
nurse, or the lending the Poor the strength they have
been temporarily deprived of by their sufferings.

It is essential, therefore, that you yourself, to be
qualified for your duties, should be always strong ; and
in the cultivation of strength and endurance, you will
find a personal reward unequalled by any other thing in
the world.   Do not undertake more than you can do,
nor give way to enthusiasm.   In the first place if you
over-tire yourself there will be a reaction, and in your
temporary weakness you will become disheartened.
Enthusiasm brings disillusionment.   Neither go among
the Poor when you are cross or ill-tempered.   As your
work is absolutely voluntary, you have no need to go
among the Poor unless when you are prepared to lend
them your strength, willingly and cheerfully.   Do not
talk to anybody about your work—that is a form of
weakness whereby we desire to get full credit for our
good works from our friends ; but in this case it is the
Poor who will reward you, in addition to the satisfaction
you will have at seeing the progress of your work.
There is nothing more just than that it is the person
who receives a benefit whose secret the transaction
should become ; and the Poor will talk plenty of your
good deeds.   Your business will soon become known ;
it cannot hide.   All in your neighbourhood will know,
and all whose acquaintance you cultivate for the
services they may be able to render you, will know.
Let that be enough of publicity.   Do not talk about
your work as a duty, do not look upon it as such.
When you begin to talk and think so, you are tiring of
it, and losing strength.   Think always of it as a pleasure,
one you would like to pursue further if you had the
strength, one that, like the gymnasium, is a good
exercise for your strength and endurance, and, therefore,

one that is enjoyable in proportion to the strength and endurance you bring to meet it.

The next stage in the education of the Poor is co-operation. When the honest Poor have had experience, how by help and encouragement to face the difficulties of their lives, they will practise helping each other, without calling on the services of the philanthropist. Having learned that it is only temporary strength they require, this they can supply to each other as occasion necessitates. Conjoined with the pleasure or helping each other, the helpers will take every care that they require no assistance themselves, and so because help is everywhere no one will seek it, if possible. When this stage is reached, and taking for granted that the better classes are progressing in strength equally with the Poor, we will have attained to the Natural conditions, as far as civilisation will allow us, from which we have departed, namely, that everybody should bear their own burdens, without inflicting trouble and annoyance upon their neighbours.

What sort of society shall we then have when the honest Poor have succeeded in contending with the difficulties of their lives, with no more than natural assistance? There will be no charity for the undeserving Poor to live upon. They, too, whether they like it or not, must bear the burden of their own lives. In such a case, by Natural law they will make these burdens as light as possible. However little it may be at first, they will work, and tiring of the too fine economy of a small wage, they will work more and more until they reach their capacity of continuous labour. They will then rank as industrious Poor, and begin to gather strength with them, merge into them, and march with them. For the first time the industrious Poor will become a class ; not with social laws, rivalries,

and social morality, but in so far as there will be a broad
line of demarcation between them and the idle and lazy,
and this line they will have a natural instinct in keeping
as well defined as possible. Not so, however, those who
are outside of it. It will confer upon them a greater
prominence than they care to accept. None of them
are strong enough to endure the reputation of being
called pariahs. They, too, will seek refuge among the
workers, and become workers with them. Hitherto
the undeserving poor have flourished, because neither
society nor civilisation could distinguish between them
and the honest, but when we have secured the
honest Poor from distress, then the others will find
their occupation gone. There will be no beggars, no
tramps, no street singers or other nuisances. The
submerged tenth will then only consist of those who
have a legitimate occupation, and can make a living as
odd jobmen. And, last of all, the drunkard will fall into
line also. Not the old and debilitated of the present
age, whose only hope is to drink themselves into their
graves comfortably ; but as the young gather strength
they will have less need for stimulants, and as their
need for it becomes less, its deterrents will appear more
formidable ; when their need for it is not very great, its
expensiveness will strike them as too unequal to its
service, and a disinclination will grow in them against
it, until they feel they can do wholly without it.

There are only two ways of contending with distress ;
by purchasing freedom from it ; or by striving with it
and conquering it. As the former is the system upon
which civilisation is based, it is not to be wondered an
that her philosophers cannot think outside of their own
condition of life, and its habits. Within a few days of
each other, lately, a Conservative statesman, a Radical
leader, a Nonconformist clergyman, and a Labour
agitator have all made public their various panaceas

for industrial and social distress. There is a family resemblance in the principles of them all, the details alone giving them their differentiation. They all in various forms subsidise the able-bodied workmen, relieve them of the expenses of bringing up their children, and reward them for their incapacity to provide for themselves at any time of their lives, by providing wholly for them in their old age. Thus from the cradle to the grave, the industrial classes are to be supported beyond their own powers of production. Whether this is done by the various suggestions of artificial wages, government grants and exemptions, or direct spoliation, does not matter to the workman. His business in future will be to create distress, so as to increase his subsidy, and the evil will become greater instead of less. On the other hand, to be able to avoid the manufacture of it, and to contend with that which is unavoidable, all that each individual requires is a little strength.

THE END.

RICHARD CLAY AND SONS, LIMITED, LONDON AND BUNGAY.

WORKS BY CHARLES BOOTH.

LIFE AND LABOUR OF THE PEOPLE IN LONDON.

4 vols. Vol. I. East, Central, and South London. Vol. II. Streets and Population Classified. Vol. III. Blocks of Buildings, Schools, and Immigration. Vol. IV. The Trades of East London. Crown 8vo, 3s. 6d. each. (Case of Five accompanying Maps. Crown 8vo, 5s.)

TIMES.—"Mr. Booth's survey has all the charm and vividness that he modestly anticipates for it. It is no less stimulating than a traveller's description of a strange country and people."

DAILY NEWS.—"Full of suggestion for the modern realistic novel writer, and of material for the historian of the future."

GUARDIAN.—"No one ought to form, much less express, an opinion about immigration, whether alien or from the country districts, without a careful study of these essays. They ought to dissipate many of the errors with which the whole subject seems surrounded."

LIFE AND LABOUR OF THE PEOPLE OF LONDON.

Volumes V. and VI. Population Classified by Trades. 7s. 6d. net each volume.

DAILY NEWS.—"Mr. Charles Booth has published, in two new volumes, more results of his patient, elaborate inquiry into the conditions of life and labour among the people of London. They are full of interesting facts. Dip into them anywhere, and you will find something to please the curious mind about actual life in London."

STANDARD.—"The fifth and sixth volumes of Mr. Charles Booth's encyclopædic work on the *Life and Labour of People in London*, just issued by Messrs. Macmillan, are quite up to the high level of previous instalments. The facts are as carefully collected and digested, and the conclusions arrived at as sound, as the notoriously uncertain character of statistics will permit. . . . It is not too much to say that the treatise, when completed by the addition of two more volumes, will rank with the best social histories of any city, while it will stand alone as the disinterested labour of a private individual who had the courage to face and deal with the industrial statistics of the greatest metropolis in the world."

PAUPERISM: A PICTURE, AND THE ENDOW-MENT OF OLD AGE: AN ARGUMENT. Crown 8vo, 5s. Popular Edition. 6d.

SPECTATOR.—"This most instructive book."

PALL MALL GAZETTE.—"Mr. Booth's present book is much more than statistical. It is an actual, living picture of that terrible drift into the pauper class, which drink, vice, and improvidence in some cases, but in others sheer unavoidable misfortune, overwhelming circumstances, or the infirmities of age, make the fate of a million and a half of English people. The narratives are not less but rather more tragic, because they are set out with the scientific plainness which we associate with the records of a pathological society."

LANCET.—"It is one of the conspicuous merits of a book like this that it conveys to the public mind a sense of the nature and shortcomings of the available information, and tends thereby to direct discussion along the lines that may be usefully followed. This is eminently true of the statistical material which is here treated."

THE AGED POOR IN ENGLAND AND WALES—CONDITION. Extra crown 8vo, 8s. 6d. net.

TIMES.—"An immense repertory of facts."

DAILY NEWS.—"Mr. Charles Booth has completed another of those remarkable books on the Life of the Poor which will give him an enduring name in the social history of this country."

STANDARD.—"What the observations and calculations of Kepler were to astronomy, Mr. Charles Booth's patient collation of facts will, we trust, prove to be to the department of social science which he has made his own."

MACMILLAN AND CO., LONDON.

MACMILLAN AND CO.'S BOOKS FOR
STUDENTS OF ECONOMICS.

SOCIAL EVOLUTION. By BENJAMIN KIDD. New and
Cheaper Edition (Fourteenth thousand), revised, with a New Preface. Crown
8vo, 5s. net.

THE EVOLUTION OF INDUSTRY. By HENRY DYER
C.E., M.A., D.Sc. 8vo, 10s. net.

ECONOMIC CLASSICS.

Edited by Prof. W. J. ASHLEY. Globe 8vo.

SELECT CHAPTERS AND PASSAGES FROM THE
"WEALTH OF NATIONS" OF ADAM SMITH, 1776. 3s. net.

THE FIRST SIX CHAPTERS OF THE "PRINCIPLES
OF POLITICAL ECONOMY AND TAXATION" OF DAVID
RICARDO, 1817. 3s. net.

PARALLEL CHAPTERS FROM THE FIRST AND
SECOND EDITIONS OF "AN ESSAY ON THE PRINCIPLE OF
POPULATION." By T. R. MALTHUS, 1798-1803. 3s. net.

ENGLAND'S TREASURE BY FORRAIGN TRADE. By
THOMAS MUN, 1664. 3s. net.

HONEST MONEY. By ARTHUR J. FONDA. Crown 8vo.
3s. 6d. net.

THE AMERICAN COMMERCIAL POLICY. Three
Historical Essays by UGO RABBENO. Second Edition. 8vo. 12s. net.

ASPECTS OF THE SOCIAL PROBLEM. By Various
Writers. Edited by BERNARD BOSANQUET. Crown 8vo, 2s. 6d. net.

DICTIONARY OF POLITICAL ECONOMY. Edited by
R. H. INGLIS PALGRAVE, F.R.S. Vol. I. (A–E). Medium 8vo,
21s. net.

PRINCIPLES OF ECONOMICS. By ALFRED MARSHALL,
M.A. Two Vols. Vol. I. Third Edition. 8vo, 12s. 6d. net.

ELEMENTS OF THE ECONOMICS OF INDUSTRY.
Being the first volume of "Elements of Economics." By Prof. A. MARSHALL.
Crown 8vo, 3s. 6d.

THE PRINCIPLES OF POLITICAL ECONOMY. By
HENRY SIDGWICK. Second Edition. 8vo, 16s.

PUBLIC FINANCE. By C. F. BASTABLE, M.A., LL.D.
Second Edition, Revised and Enlarged. 8vo, 12s. 6d. net.

By the late Prof. W. STANLEY JEVONS, LL.D, F.R.S.

THE STATE IN RELATION TO LABOUR. New Edition.
Crown 8vo, 2s. 6d.

POLITICAL ECONOMY. Pott 8vo, 1s.

THE THEORY OF POLITICAL ECONOMY. Third
Edition. 8vo, 10s. 6d.

INVESTIGATIONS IN CURRENCY AND FINANCE.
Illustrated by Twenty Diagrams. Edited with an Introduction by Prof. H. S.
FOXWELL. 8vo, 21s.

INTRODUCTION TO THE STUDY OF POLITICAL
ECONOMY. By LUIGI COSSA. Revised by the Author and translated by
LOUIS DYER, M.A. Crown 8vo, 8s. 6d. net.

MACMILLAN AND CO., LONDON.

MACMILLAN AND CO.'S BOOKS FOR:
STUDENTS OF ECONOMICS.

AN INTRODUCTION TO THE THEORY OF VALUE, on the lines of Menger, Wieser, and Böhm-Bawerk. By DR. WILLIAM SMART. Crown 8vo, 3s. net.

NATURAL VALUE. By FRIEDRICH VON WIESER. Edited, with a Preface and Analysis, by DR. WILLIAM SMART 8vo, 10s. net.

By Prof. EUGENE V. BÖHM-BAWERK.

CAPITAL AND INTEREST. A Critical History of Economical Theory. Translated with a Preface and Analysis by WILLIAM SMART, LL.D. 8vo, 12s. net.

THE POSITIVE THEORY OF CAPITAL. Translated with a Preface and Analysis by DR. WILLIAM SMART. 8vo, 12s. net.

THE ALPHABET OF ECONOMIC SCIENCE. By PHILIP H. WICKSTEED. Part I. Elements of the Theory of Value or Worth. With Diagrams. Globe 8vo, 2s. 6d.

THE JOINT STANDARD : a Plain Exposition of Monetary Principles and of the Monetary Controversy. By ELIJAH HELM. Crown 8vo, 3s. 6d. net.

EIGHT HOURS FOR WORK. By JOHN RAE, M.A., Author of "Contemporary Socialism." Crown 8vo, 4s. 6d. net.

THE DISTRIBUTION OF WEALTH. By JOHN R. COMMONS, Professor of Economics and Social Science, Indiana University. 8vo, 7s. net.

PROFIT SHARING BETWEEN EMPLOYER AND EMPLOYEE. By N. P. GILMAN. Crown 8vo, 7s. 6d.

SOCIALISM AND THE AMERICAN SPIRIT. By N. P. GILMAN. Crown 8vo, 6s. 6d.

THE UNEMPLOYED. By GEOFFREY DRAGE, Secretary to the Labour Commission. Crown 8vo, 3s. 6d. net.

THE CONFLICT OF CAPITAL AND LABOUR HISTORICALLY AND ECONOMICALLY CONSIDERED. Being a History and Review of the Trade Unions of Great Britain. By GEORGE HOWELL. Second and Revised Edition. Crown 8vo, 7s. 6d.

HANDY BOOK OF THE LABOUR LAWS. Third Edition, Revised. By GEORGE HOWELL. Crown 8vo, 3s. 6d. net.

By Prof. FRANCIS A. WALKER, Ph.D.

POLITICAL ECONOMY. 8vo, 12s. 6d.

A BRIEF TEXT-BOOK OF POLITICAL ECONOMY. Crown 8vo, 6s. 6d.

FIRST LESSONS IN POLITICAL ECONOMY. Crown 8vo, 5s.

THE WAGES QUESTION. A Treatise on Wages and the Wages Class. Extra Crown 8vo, 8s. 6d. net.

MONEY. Extra Crown 8vo, 8s. 6d. net.

MONEY IN ITS RELATIONS TO TRADE AND INDUSTRY. Crown 8vo, 7s. 6d.

LAND AND ITS RENT. Fcap. 8vo, 3s. 6d.

MACMILLAN AND CO., LONDON.